A LOST CLAUS

A CHRISTMAS COZY MYSTERY: BOOK THREE

MONA MARPLE

Thank you to my advance readers who help spot those pesky typos:

Nadine, Renee, Roxx, and Robin

CHRISTMAS MYSTERY BONUS

Help yourself to a festive fun pack, available exclusively at:

https://dl.bookfunnel.com/9ckxf7kcfh

Ho-ho-hope you enjoy it!

Mona x

The Claus Family Tree

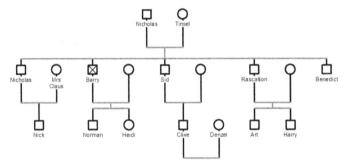

1
———

It had been a long day in the surgery, and I was half-distracted by the evening plans I had. I'd been feeling excitement and nerves about it for weeks.

Back when I had a month between me and the big moment, I'd mostly felt excited. But as the day grew closer, those nerves started to take centre stage.

A discreet glance at my watch told me that it was going to happen in less than half an hour.

Nick's relatives were in town. The whole Claus family would already be gathered and waiting for me, and I was desperate to make a good impression on every last one of them.

They were the Claus family, for Kris Kringle's sake! My nerves were natural, I knew that. That didn't make the fluttering of the butterflies in my stomach any less real.

I shook my head, tried to shake the doubts away. It was going to be a good time, and I was there for every second of it. I just hoped they all liked me.

"I felt it twinge when I hung the curtains back up, Doc," my patient said, referencing the shoulder she'd dislocated a few weeks before during a vigorous stretch to place the angel on top of her 12 foot Christmas tree.

"I'm not surprised! You shouldn't be doing things like that!" I exclaimed.

"I've never lived in an untidy house and I'm not about to start now."

"You're still recovering. You need to remember to rest, okay? Get that son of yours to help you out some. I know he wants to," I said with a grin as I handed the prescription over to my last patient of the day.

The old lady elf gave a brisk nod of her head and took the sheet of paper from me. "He doesn't do the jobs as well as I do, that's the problem."

"I know. But I bet you can train him and get him into good shape. See it as a challenge!"

"That's a jingling good idea, doc. I'll be sure to do that," the elf said, and she rose from her chair and left the surgery.

As soon as she was gone, I pulled off my white jacket and glanced at my watch. I was over my intended finish time, as normal. Patients everywhere were chatty, but the patients in Candy Cane Hollow were among the most talkative people - and elves! - I'd ever come across.

Most appointments started with ten minutes of the patient enquiring as to how I was, how Nick was, how Mrs Claus and Father Christmas were, and how I felt about whatever festive event was coming up next. I suspected that some of the younger patients even faked illness so that they could get me alone and ask whether they were on the nice list or not!

By the time we got to discuss medical issues, some patients had even forgotten why they had made the appointment in the first place. In fact, I swore that some of them made regular appointments more as a social commitment than because of any great medical need, not that that was unique to Candy Cane Hollow.

The result? I was constantly running late as I went from patient to patient in my surgery and at scattered home visits throughout the festive town.

But nobody minded. Patients were always pleased to see me, and several of them brought food in for me. The surgery was always rich in biscuit assortments and homemade cakes. I never had to plan ahead and pack lunch.

I had to admit, it was a huge change of pace from my days working as a locum GP in London, where every day had targets attached to it, and every minute was tracked and scrutinised. Not to mention where the complaints about being kept waiting seemed endless.

As I pushed my arm into my winter coat, the phone on my desk rang. I had moved to answer it before I even realised. No matter the time, I wouldn't let a patient's call go unanswered, and my receptionist had clocked off some time ago at my insistence.

"Dr Wood speaking, how can I help?"

"Oh, hello, Dr Wood! It's only me, I'm sorry to trouble you since I expect you're busy with important work all day," the caller launched straight into their chatter.

"Gilbert?" I recognised the dramatic, nasal tones of the elf who served as housekeeper at Claus Cottage.

"Ah, you remember my name! I'm honoured. I'm just calling to let you know that the first batch of miniature roast dinners will be out of the oven in precisely four minutes, and yet you're not here."

"I'm sorry! My patients ran over. I was just leaving before you rang."

"A likely story. Please don't lie on my account. Holly, is it that you detest my cooking?"

"What? Of course not!"

"I have half a mind to hang up my apron and apply for Elf Benefits, I really do. I prepare food and nobody turns up!"

A commotion in the background at his end of the line distracted me.

"Nobody's turned up?"

"Well, sure, the others are all here. But you're not, and that empty seat at the table will sure spark rumours. It's the sign of a bad domestic elf, you know, when people start arriving at events after the food has been served. Oh! The shame of it! My family will never... it's three minutes now, by the way."

"Okay, Gilbert, let's talk about all of this later. Let me hang up and I'll come right away."

"Oh, sure, you want to hang up! Much more important things to do than speak to Gilbert!"

"Gilbert, I need to hang up so that I can come over and taste your delicious food. Are you doing those little York-shire puddings with the roast dinner inside? You know I love those!"

"You're saying that because I just told you that's what I've made! Don't flatter me, if you'd rather eat yellow snow than my lovingly prepared food, just say!"

"Oh, Gilly, come on..."

He sniffed at the other end of the line and I heard Mrs Claus' sweet voice ask who he was speaking to.

"I'll leave you to it," Gilbert said, and ended the call.

I shook my head and laughed to myself. Gilbert had been threatening to walk out of his job on a daily basis ever since I'd met him. There was always some tiny thing that caused him to take offence and catastrophize.

I locked up and made the short journey through the

snow, past cute cottages where I could see the glow of fires and hear the bustle of families excited for the approach of Christmas. I continued to crunch my way up to Claus Cottage. The beautiful home was nestled on a hill overlooking the whole of Candy Cane Hollow, and was trimmed year-round with festive lights and decorations.

The front of the cottage was busy with parked up vehicles that I didn't realise, and I felt another burst of nerves as I squeezed in between the sleighs and cars and stomped across the snow.

As I approached the house, I saw a shape in the front doorway and felt my stomach flip as I realised who was waiting for me.

"Nick!" I exclaimed, and I ran the last few steps to him and threw myself at him, burying myself into his warmth. He smelled like cocoa and cinnamon and the last embers of a burning fire, and his arms felt like home.

"Hey, you. Good day?" He asked. I peeled myself away from him and saw his dimpled cheek, his brown-pools-of-honey eyes. I leaned in and planted a soft kiss on his full lips.

As I pulled back from him, I saw the net curtain of the den twitch, and Mrs Claus quickly hide out of sight. She somehow managed to witness every one of our kisses and celebrated each one for us.

"It's been great! How are things here? I'm sorry I couldn't come earlier and help get things ready," I said as Nick opened the door and led me inside.

"Oh, it's fine. You know Gilbert wouldn't have let you anywhere near any jobs. He's been even more sensitive than normal today."

"It's a big day," I said, plastering a big grin on my face to hopefully hide my nerves.

"They're going to love you," Nick reassured me as we entered the wide entrance hall. He took my coat from me and hung it with the others; the coat stand wobbled under the weight of so many outer garments.

"I hope so," I said. "Meeting your family is a big deal. I hope I don't do anything wrong."

"You could never do anything wrong. Just be yourself," Nick encouraged, and with those words of wisdom he pushed open the door to the den and I felt my heart race as a room full of people all turned and looked at me.

"Here she is!"

"Is this her?"

"She looks alright, Nick!"

"Finally he's brought a woman home, eh! We were thinking he was..."

"He was what?"

"Guys, guys! I'd like to introduce you all to Holly!" Nick said.

I scanned around the room and wondered how I would ever remember everyone's names.

The Claus family were mainly men, and they were sprawling around in the den, clearly feeling right at home. Not that that was a surprise. I remembered how welcome Mrs Claus had made me feel when I'd first arrived. Of course these blood relatives would feel right at ho-ho-home.

"I'm so glad to get to meet you all before you set off for the big ice fishing trip in the morning," I tried to project my voice but the group were rowdy.

"Let's do introductions," Nick whispered to me. He placed his hand on the small of my back as he guided me around the room, and I felt my body tingle at his touch.

"We'll start with the fairest of them all. This is my cousin Heidi. She's easy to remember as the only girl."

"Hey Holly! Finally, someone's brave enough to try to take on the next Santa. Oh, and I'm a woman, not a girl, Nicholas," she corrected.

Nick's cheeks flushed with colour. "Of course. Sorry! You're still that blonde haired kid with grass stains on your jeans in my memory."

"It's actually a way that the patriarchy controls females, by infantilising them and never allowing them to grow up."

"Oh, be quiet, Heidi," another female called across the room and I felt myself relax a little as I realised that Ginger Rumples, Nick's oldest friend, was present.

To my surprise, Heidi took Ginger's comment well. She stuck her tongue out but then grinned at me and offered her hand. "Welcome to the family. You're punching above your weight, Nick."

"I know," Nick said, and he seemed to relax a little too as he heard his cousin's approval.

"So, Heidi is my uncle Barry's daughter. We lost Barry far too young. This chap here is Barry's son, Norman."

Norman was a tall and slender man with a whisper of a moustache above his top lip, so faint it was as if he hadn't quite committed to the idea of growing one. "Good day."

"Hi!" I responded, complete with an awkward little wave.

Nick led me on.

"Over here we have Clive and his husband, Denzel. Clive is Uncle Sid's son."

My head was already a mass of names. "I'll never remember all of these names!"

Clive raised a glass of Champagne to me and laughed. "Don't worry about it, babe. Denzel had the exact same problem. There are far too many of us Clauses! We have to make sure the family doesn't die out, of course."

"I joke that they're like the Royal Family, always thinking of succession," Denzel leaned in and winked at me.

"That's enough out of you pair," Nick teased and moved me on. "Now here's Uncle Rascal!"

Rascal had a black Mohawk and wore a leather jacket with spikes adorning the sleeves. He didn't look so much festive as like an ageing punk rocker.

He reached out and pulled me in for a hug, and his breath burned like whisky.

"Alright, let's take a look at you! Not bad, not bad. You ever get bored of Nick here, come and give me your number, alright?"

"Come on..." Nick protested.

"What? I'm a red-blooded man. I can't apologise for liking the ladies, and the ladies shouldn't have to apologise for liking me!"

I laughed.

"Where are your boys at?" Nick asked his uncle.

Rascal gave a shrug. "Tell them to bring me another drink if you find them."

"Ah, here's Harry!" Nick exclaimed and pulled me away from Rascal eagerly.

Harry, freckled and ginger, winced as we approached. "What did dad say?"

"Nothing worse than you'd imagine," Nick said. "Anyway, I wanted to make sure Holly got to meet the boy wonder. This kid's a genius. Heading off to Cambridge this year to study... what is it again?"

"I'm reading law. I'm going to be a barrister," Harry's slender chest inflated with pride.

"That's amazing!" I gushed.

"And I hear you're a doctor?" Harry asked.

I gave a slight nod, embarrassed to be defined by my

profession. It always made me feel conflicted, that my job might be the most interesting thing about me.

"Where's Art?" Nick asked.

"Oh, he'll be in a corner somewhere," Harry said.

We moved on, and located the last person I had to greet. Art was indeed in a corner, literally sitting on the floor, his nose buried in a book.

"Comfy?" Nick teased.

Art jumped up to his feet and stared at me, but said nothing.

"I'm Holly," I said after a few moments had passed.

He nodded, gave a nervous smile and held out his hand. I shook it and felt how clammy his dark skin was. His long black hair trailed past his shoulders.

"What are you reading?" I asked.

"Oh!" He exclaimed, and held the cover out. It was some sci fi novel, the cover emblazoned with a spacecraft and exploding meteorites. "It's really excellent. I was outside the shop an hour before it opened on release day. I was on the fan Wiki and there was a rumour there was a signed copy, just hidden with the normal stock. I don't know if that was true or not. I didn't get it, if it was. Maybe one of the staff got it before the shop opened. It would have been quite the talking point!"

"I can imagine," I said. I enjoyed reading and, even if sci fi wasn't my genre of choice, I could appreciate a fellow bookworm's love of the written word.

"We'll let you get back to it," Nick said with a wink.

He led me out into the quiet hallway and grinned at me. He was like a child sometimes, and it struck me then that he was waiting with baited breath for my opinion on his family.

"They're all lovely, Nick," I said. "Those last two boys - they're brothers? They look nothing like each other."

"They have different mums. Rascal never settled down. In fact, I wouldn't be surprised if he has a few more children out there with women who never tracked him down."

"His name's fitting then! Your uncles all have traditional names, and then there's Rascal."

"That's my grandmother's influence. The first born always has to be Nicholas, of course. And my grandfather was a big fan of tradition, but granny was different. She was quite laidback and fun. And her own name was a bit out there. She was called Tinsel."

"Tinsel?" I repeated.

"I don't believe you can judge, Holly Wood..." he said with a laugh.

We returned to the den just as Gilbert appeared, platters in hand.

I inhaled and savoured the aroma of gravy, cranberry sauce and turkey.

"Gilbert! You've outdone yourself!" I complimented the sensitive elf as he approached.

His cheeks flushed and he eyed me. "What does that mean? Are you surprised that I can knock up mini roasts?"

"Not at all!" I objected.

"Come on Gilly, relax," Nick soothed.

"Forgive me, Nick. My head's all over the place today. I know how much these family get togethers mean to you all! And this one especially!"

"Why this one especially?" I asked.

"Well, it's your first one, Holly! You're being welcomed to the family! And I don't know about you, but if that was me, being paraded around in front of literally the most powerful family in the whole entire world, I'd be - no exaggeration - absolutely petrified. In fact, that's the whole reason I rang you. I wanted to make sure you hadn't done a runner. Check you were still going to go through with it all..." Gilbert chattered maniacally until his attention returned to the platter. "Goodness gumdrops! These won't be at the perfect temperature to serve if I stand here listening to you two gossip! Excuse me!"

And with that, he pushed his way into the den, where the crowd greeted him and the food with a hungry appreciation.

"Well," Nick said, then stopped, unsure of how to continue the sentence.

"He's right, Nick. You're the Claus family! Goodness gumdrops, I think I forget sometimes. Can I really do this? How can I possibly impress the Claus family?"

Nick gave me a lazy grin and the dimple in his cheek smiled at me. "Miss Wood, you've been doing nothing but impress us since you arrived in town."

Despite myself, I felt my cheeks flush and my confidence increase a little.

"Well?"

"Well indeed. After that pep talk, we should get back in there," I said, hoping my voice wasn't shaking as much as my hands were.

Nick reached for me and pulled me close to him. Something about the intensity of his gaze made me fear that I may actually swoon and collapse into his arms.

"Just so you know, there's only one person with an opinion that matters, and you've already won him over," he purred into my ear and I felt my whole body blush.

"Well, thank you, Mr Claus," I said with a light tone, needing to cool things down if I had any chance of going back in the den and chatting to his family. "But we all know the person with the opinion who matters is your mother."

Nick grinned and the dimple in his cheek grinned at me too. I'd never tire of seeing that dimple. "Touché."

"How dare you?!" A voice shouted from the den.

Nick cringed as he led me back in to check on things. "Welcome to the family."

In the centre of the room, Norman had squared up in front of Rascal, who sat in a wingback chair with a smirk on his face.

"Calm down, old boy. Don't spoil the family reunion," Rascal said as he accepted a mini roast from the platter.

"Me? I'm not the one spoiling anything. How dare you say that about my father? Take it back right now! I insist!" Norman shrieked.

"Or what?" Rascal asked with a raised eyebrow. A trail of gravy dribbled down his chin, unnoticed.

"Dad..." Harry warned.

"I'm just joking, son. That's what families are meant to do with each other, but Norman here doesn't seem like he got the memo about that. Lighten up, eh, Norm?"

Nick groaned beside me. "Here we go."

"Now, you boys cut it out. We're all family and we're going to have a wonderful time together. You hear me, dears?" Mrs Claus crossed into the middle of the room, folded her arms across her bosom and eyed each of the group in turn.

"Too many men, that's the problem," Heidi said with a smile.

"I couldn't possibly comment on that, dear, considering that my two favourite people in the world are both of the masculine variety," Mrs Claus said with a wink.

I watched as Heidi grinned. Mrs Claus really did have the ability to calm any confrontation, it seemed.

"Now, I'd like to make a toast if I may," Father Christmas himself stood and raised his glass.

The energy in the room shifted minutely as each person stood slightly more to attention.

"After Christmas itself, this is my favourite occasion each year. To be joined in Claus Cottage, the home of generations of the Claus family, with not only my family, but my brothers and their families. It is truly magical. We are not complete in number this year, and it wouldn't be appropriate to continue without mentioning the people who can't be with us. Our parents, of course, who gave us such idyllic childhoods in this very home. May they live on in eternal festivity. Next, my brother, Barry, taken too young."

"Taken too young," the crowd repeated, gazes cast down to the ground.

"My brother Sid sends his best wishes. His medical research is at a vital point and we sacrifice our time with him gladly so that the world can benefit from his talent and hard work. And my brother Benedict, too ill to join us this year. His absence does at least open up the space for someone else to take second place in our ice fishing competition."

"I'm after first place and nothing less!" Rascal shouted, his words full of liquor and jumbled.

"You say that every year and most of the time you're too blotto to even get the line in the hole," Norman said, his lips pursed. He didn't seem as quick to move past the fall out as everyone else.

"Everyone knows only FC can take a first place," Clive said with a grin.

"Would you be complimenting me in a bid to get that new hover-board that's on your list, Clive?" Father Christmas teased.

Denzel folded his arms and gave his husband an astonished look. "I thought we'd agreed they're too dangerous? It's not even a regulated industry yet."

Clive gave a nervous laugh. "I'll be careful, I promise."

"You said that when you wanted to run with reindeer too, remember?"

"Oh, that was just a little scratch!"

"Moving on!" Father Christmas' booming voice continued, as Clive nestled himself into his husband and murmured an apology in his ear. "As sad as I am to not see the faces of those not with us, I am equally delighted to see all of you who are here. Each and every one of you are dear to me, and so, I raise a toast, to the Claus family!"

"To the Claus family, dear," Mrs Claus said.

"To the Claus family!" Everyone else sang out in unison.

"And let us not forget our very talented Gilbert, who takes care of us all so well and caters these events to a standard that amazes me each and every time!" Mrs Claus continued.

Gilbert turned from the doorway and faced the room, his cheeks flushed and his eyes watery.

"I don't know what to say, Mrs Claus," his voice trembled as he spoke.

"You don't have to say anything!" Rascal shouted.

"No, of course," Gilbert said with mild disappointment, then left the room to fetch more food.

"Nice elf, good chef, but boy he can talk," Rascal said.

"He's part of the family, dear, why shouldn't he talk?" Mrs Claus asked.

Rascal rolled his eyes but said nothing to challenge her.

Heidi caught my eye and came over to me, her blonde hair tucked behind her ears.

"How are you finding all this? It's a lot, right?"

"Oh, I..."

"I mean, all these men. The whole first born son thing. The lineage. It's an institution more than a family, right?"

"Oh, well... erm. I don't know about that. I was sorry to hear of you losing your dad. That must have been tough."

"Of course it was."

"Do you still have your mum?"

Heidi shrugged. "I guess. It turns out being *a* Mrs Claus but not *the* Mrs Claus isn't really that attractive an offer. My mum never took the name, of course. She was a feminist. She still is. I see her every now and then."

"That's good. I have to admit, all of this is new to me. Candy Cane Hollow and all this. It's a lot to take in."

"And you're a doctor?" Heidi asked.

I nodded.

To my horror, Heidi raised her hand and performed a high five on me, complete with a high-pitched whoop.

"Right on! Sisters are doing it for themselves! That's awesome. What do you specialise in?"

"I don't. I'm a GP," I explained.

"Ah. Okay. Well, I mean, that's still not bad though. Good for you."

"Thanks," I forced myself to say.

"I hope you're playing nicely, Hi?" Nick asked.

"You know me, Santa. Always on the nice list."

"Huh, I won't comment on that. What was happening with your brother and Rascal?"

Heidi rolled her eyes. "Rascal was being Rascal, of course. Made a pretty low dig about dad, but you know how Norman is. He's so tightly wound up, he's always ready to snap."

"Rascal's drunk. Norman should just ignore him," Nick said.

"Rascal's always drunk, Nicholas, and let me remind you that a man's drunken actions are still actions that affect others. For too long, we - and I mean women especially - have excused or allowed behaviour from men because the man was drunk or ignorant or whatever."

"Is this from your studies?"

Heidi nodded and her pale cheeks flushed pink. "I'm working on dissertation ideas."

"What are you studying?" I asked.

"Feminism, patriarchy. Gender studies, I guess you could call it. I challenged the University on their male-focused curricula so they allowed me to build my own course. It's endlessly fascinating. A strong independent woman like you, Holly, you'd love it. In fact..."

"What?" I asked, intrigued despite myself.

"No, it's not my place."

"What?"

"Well, it just occurred to me. Maybe if you'd had access to this course, you might have had the self-belief to push yourself and choose a specialism."

"Huh!" I said, too stunned to add anything additional.

Heidi leaned in so close to me that I could count her individual eye lashes. "We need women surgeons."

And with that, she turned and moved away to speak to someone else.

"Wow. I feel like I just had a catch up with my careers advisor and she's thoroughly disappointed in me," I joked.

"Nobody could ever be disappointed in you, Holly, dear. Now, Nick. Your cousin Norman is feeling a bit down in the dumps. You really should go over and rally him along a bit," Mrs Claus said. She rubbed my arm as she spoke.

"I don't think I'm the best person for that, mum. I wouldn't know what to say," Nick squirmed.

"Nonsense. Go on, there's a good boy."

"I'll come with you," I offered.

We approached Norman, who stood at the far edge of the room, looking out of the window on to the snowscape outside.

Nick cleared his throat and Norman turned.

"Mummy sent you over, has she?" Norman asked.

"Yep," Nick admitted, and the two seemed to relax.

"Glad that you brought this fine lady over to protect you. Holly, isn't it? Tell me, what did this oaf do to impress a lady like you?"

"Oh," I felt my cheeks flush and heard a childish giggle emerge from my mouth.

"I think she's only interested in my mother, let's be honest. Anyway, how are you doing? You seem a little, erm..."

"On edge? Sick of that drunk mess getting to turn up and live another day when my dad doesn't get to?"

"That's a fair summary. You want to talk?"

"To you?" Norman raised his eyebrows.

"I was thinking more like a professional. You know, here in Candy Cane Hollow we have a 24/7 phone line. Serenity Services. It's all confidential."

"It's tough losing a parent. No shame in needing to talk about it with someone trained," I said.

Norman looked at me, assessed me. "You've been through it?"

I couldn't answer, couldn't get my mouth to form the word that would mean yes, my mother was dead. I nodded instead, felt my eyes fill. Nick reached for my hand.

"Gosh, I'm sorry. Your mum or dad?"

"Mum," I forced myself to say.

Norman let out a long whistle. "You know, I have this

theory, that it's worse for sons to lose dads and daughters to lose mums. I don't know if it's true. I know I've struggled with losing dad more than Heidi did. She's a year older, but I don't know if that one year would make a difference."

"I think part of Heidi considers every male death to be correcting the balance a little," Nick said, then cringed as he heard how his words sounded.

Norman did a double take, then broke into laughter and slapped a heavy hand on Nick's back. "Man! That's it! That's it man! Everyone seems to tiptoe around me now. I love that you just said it like it is! I love my sister, but I can't wait for her to outgrow this phase."

"You think her... erm... feminism's a phase?" I asked.

Norman grinned at me. "I see Heidi twice a year maybe, and every time I do, there's a new obsession. Last summer it was all about succession and bloodlines. She had a stint all about climate change. Now it's feminism. She's a woman who needs a cause to fight for."

"Sounds like she's trying to fill a hole."

"I've said the exact same thing to my... to my dad, when he was still with us."

"I really am sorry for your loss, Norman. I know you've heard that so many times over the years and it doesn't change anything, but I don't know if I was brave enough to ever come up and say it to you. So I'm saying it now," Nick said.

"I appreciate it. You always were my favourite cousin, you know, and not because of the Santa gig."

Nick grinned. "I've had a soft spot for you, too. It's why we fought... we were closer than we were to the others."

"You guys fought?" I asked.

"We fought like cats and dogs growing up. Nick's a bit older..."

"Four years older!" Nick clarified with mock pride in his voice.

"Alright, four years older, and our dads would send us off to play and he'd try to lose me and leave me behind!"

"Remember that one year I convinced you that snowmen were really alive?"

"I didn't sleep for weeks!" Norman laughed at the memory.

"That's mean!" I exclaimed, and pretended to dig my elbow in to Nick.

"I was actually just ahead of my time. They've since found a line of wild snowmen," Nick said.

I turned to him with a grin, but his expression was serious.

I allowed that to sink in for a moment. Wild snowmen?!

"But at the time, you were just being mean, Nick. You need to hear this before you commit to him, Holly. See the man he really is," Norman said, with a wink.

Gilbert appeared at my side. "Pigs in blankets?"

"Ooh! Yes please," I enthused, grabbed three, and passed one along each to Nick and Norman.

I ate hungrily and slower than necessary, unsure of what else I could say to Norman.

I didn't need to worry. He grabbed a second pig in blanket from the tray and moved away from us.

"Are things okay between you and Norman now?" I asked Nick.

Nick shrugged. "He changed when he lost his dad. He closed himself off, didn't come to any family get togethers for a good while. I don't really feel like I know him that well any more. It's like he has this whole life I don't know about now."

"That's a shame. You get on with everyone else?"

"Of course! They're family, I love them. And it's really great to see them. In fact, it's nice to see them, and it's nice to have them go back to their own houses again too. Is that awful to admit?"

I thought of my sister, August. She was younger than me, with her handsome husband, adorable toddler son, and picturesque country cottage. Her whole life was sorted, and even though she was my best friend, being around her perfect life could be exhausting.

The key was not to compare her life to my own. I just needed to figure out how to do that.

"It's not awful at all," I said as Nick planted a kiss on my forehead.

"Are you sure I can't convince you to come along with us tomorrow?" Nick murmured in my ear.

I giggled and pulled away a little. "I'd be worse than useless out there. Anyway, I have all of these plans to work on with your mum."

"I know. It's just, you've been so busy with work. I kind of hate that we'll be spending a few days apart."

I felt my heart thump in my chest. "Me too. But you'll be back before you know it."

"Well, excuse us if we're interrupting!" Clive exclaimed as he and Denzel approached. Denzel gave me a smile and I returned it.

"Hello there," I said.

"We just came across to ask whether we should be buying hats for the wedding," Clive asked.

Denzel rolled his eyes. "Leave them alone. Tonight might put Holly off this family completely."

"True! Lord knows, D was ready to run for the hills. He only stuck around because I'm a love machine," Clive said with a wink.

"I call you many things behind your back, but a love machine is not one of them," Denzel deadpanned.

"Don't play too hard to get, sugar, or I might stop trying. Now, Nick, what's going on with Art?"

I followed Clive's gaze over to the corner of the room, where Art remained on the floor, his treasured book in front of his face.

"It looks like he's really engrossed in that book," I said with a smile.

"He's just socially awkward, Clive. Leave him alone," Nick said.

"Oh, I will! You know me, Nick, I wouldn't say gobble-gobble to a Christmas turkey. I just fear for him with Rascal. The more he drinks, the less happy he's going to be about his first born not even mingling while his brother's first born is the new Santa..."

Nick rolled his eyes but laughed. "I'm not babysitting Rascal's temper, or his drinking. If there's a problem, we'll deal with it when we get to it."

"Ooh, goodie! Holly, do your family have adventures like these?"

I smiled. "There aren't enough of us. But we have our share of issues, like every family does."

"I don't know why some of these meat suits get invited back year after year! At least my dad's invitation got lost in the post!"

"I thought he was too busy to come?" Nick asked.

"He is, I'm only joking. We all know that daddy's on a mission to save the world!"

"Good for him. But this weekend, the only mission I'm on is to catch an enormous fish!" Nick chuckled.

We had entered the den and it was empty, although not as neat as Gilbert usually kept it. A few half-empty mugs of cocoa sat on the coffee table, a pair of woollen gloves rested on one of the chairs, and there was a subtle stain on the rug that looked very much like mud. I didn't want to be around when Gilbert noticed *that*.

Various booming voices and banging sounds came from around the cottage, and the pipes clanged and squealed to signal that someone was in the shower.

"They've had breakfast and now they're doing final checks. Making sure all of their gear is ready. They're tremendously excited!" Mrs Claus explained.

"Have you ever been ice fishing? Is it dangerous?" I asked.

"It can be, I guess. Any activity that takes place on the frozen lakes is dangerous, dear. But the Claus family have always been ice fishers! They'll be careful."

"I'm surprised the Clauses have such a dangerous hobby," I admitted.

Mrs Claus winked. "It does inflate the life insurance payments quite a bit!"

Heavy footsteps came down the stairs and I glanced up as Nick appeared. He grinned as soon as he saw me and I swear my heart skipped a beat.

"Holly! I didn't think you'd have time to come back this morning. Wait, have you changed your mind about joining us?" Nick asked, his delight revealing the dimple in his cheek.

Mrs Claus moved away, but only a little. She wanted us to have privacy, of course. Just not too much.

"I always have time for you," I murmured, suddenly shy. Perhaps it was too sentimental to have made the journey from my small apartment above the surgery. Nick would, after all, only be gone for a few nights.

He wrapped his big arms around me and I inhaled his scent; cinnamon, cloves, red berries.

"Promise me you'll be careful out there," I whispered.

"Promise," he said, then kissed the top of my head. "You could come and supervise if you're really worried?"

I gazed up at him. "Maybe next time."

The rest of his family made their way down to the entrance hall, as if a silent alarm had gone off and notified them all that it was time to leave.

They bundled themselves and their belongings into one of the old sleighs, and a team of reindeer were fixed in place.

I watched the scene with a sense of trepidation in my stomach. Who exactly had decided that cutting a hole out of the very ice you were sitting on was a good idea?

"Chill, sis. I'm the brains on this trip," Heidi called out to me with a grin.

"Thank you!" I shouted back with a laugh, not wanting to seem like a party pooper.

"You'll miss him, dear, won't you?" Mrs Claus stood by my side, bundled into a huge cardigan decorated with knitted poinsettias.

"So much. Is that silly?" I asked as the reality of a few days away from Nick sank in.

"You know, we could do a lot of our Mistletoe Matchmakers work from out there in the cabin."

"We could?"

Mrs Claus nodded and winked at me. "Hold up there, dears! Make space for a couple of small ones to squeeze in."

The delight in Nick's eyes made me certain I'd made the right choice, even if I knew nothing about ice fishing and was more than a little scared that I might bump into a polar bear or something.

He dove out of the sleigh and grabbed me, lifted me from the floor and spun me in a circle.

I laughed and squealed until he set me back down. Mrs Claus looked giddy enough to faint.

"Gilbert, dear, pack a quick bag for Holly and I please?"

Gilbert gave a nod of his head. "Thank goodness. I'll gather a few things for myself too."

"For you, dear?"

"I've had my reservations all along about the Claus family eating out there. I know they have 'staff' out there, but I really dread to think what kind of slop they'll be serving!" The elf exclaimed, then disappeared back into Claus Cottage with a flounce.

While the extra bags were packed, there was a final check that everything was in place, and finally Gilbert emerged, somehow carrying six huge cases despite his tiny stature.

One of the cases banged and clattered as he carried it across to the sleigh.

"What do you have in there, alcohol?" Rascal shouted, hopefully.

"Goodness gumdrops, nothing of the sort. This is just a few of my kitchen essentials. I have no idea how well the pots and pans out there are washed. I'd rather not take the risk."

"You think of everything, dear," Mrs Claus flattered the elf and he grinned with pride.

Nick offered his hand and I climbed up into the sleigh next to him, with Mrs Claus stepping in after me and Gilbert on the end.

"You're wrapped up enough? It's going to get cold when this baby starts moving," Nick purred in my ear.

"I'm sure you can help keep me warm," I said, not realising how flirtatious my words came across until I'd said them, and heard Mrs Claus try to suppress a squeal of delight beside me.

"I sure will," Nick whispered, and he wrapped an arm around me.

Blankets had been laid out in the sleigh and Nick grabbed one and placed it over both me and his mum as the sleigh began to move.

Nick was right, the reindeer could really move, and as they picked up speed, the icy wind attacked any bare skin it found. Luckily, Gilbert had packed cute balaclavas for the three of us, and we all put them on. We looked like a festive group of armed robbers, but we were warm.

I gasped as we left Candy Cane Hollow and moved out into the frozen wilderness. The trees were bare stalks, leaves long gone, and the snow grew deeper and deeper.

Nick pointed out a herd of wild reindeer prancing across the frozen tundra, their dance so elegant and playful it looked choreographed.

"Now, dear, shall I get you up to speed about the Mistletoe Matchmakers event?" Mrs Claus said with a gentle rub of my arm.

"I'd love that," I said. Mrs Claus had asked me to help her with the event, but I didn't know much about it. I was just always happy to spend more time in her festive company.

"By the way, I hope you're not too busy at work, dear. How's the new receptionist working out for you?"

"Oh, Belinda's great. She really helps keep me on track," I admitted.

"That's wonderful. Now, Mistletoe Matchmakers! This event was created, Holly, because really nobody wants to be alone at Christmas."

"Well, that's true," I said. I thought back to my life before Candy Cane Hollow, and the Christmas alone that I was quickly approaching. Mrs Claus had saved me in more ways than one.

"It's really a fun night. Anyone can join in, and we sit them in pairs for two minutes. When the jingle bells ring, they get put in a different pair. And that repeats for an hour or so, then there's some time afterwards where anyone who felt a connection can stay and find their way back to the person they liked."

"It sounds wonderful," I admitted.

"Everyone leaves having gained something! For some people, they find a new friend. And others find the love of their life! Isn't that something?"

"It sure is! And the event is next week?"

Mrs Claus nodded. "It's all ready, really. I just need a co-host, and really there's nobody I'd prefer than you, dear."

I grinned. I knew exactly what she was doing. She was training me, for she had high hopes that I would be the next Mrs Claus.

"I'd love to help," I said, because I was hoping for the same thing she was.

4

We arrived at Camp Mackerel after an hour of breathtaking scenery, and the camp itself took my breath away.

"Whoa. When you were trying to convince me to come, you should really have led with this," I told Nick as I gazed at what looked like an exclusive spa hotel.

Nick shrugged. "I didn't have you down as a woman who wanted the finer things in life."

"Oh, I definitely want the finer things in life if they look like this," I teased.

Camp Mackerel was a large-scale log cabin, but the front was full height glass windows and we were greeted by a valet who offered to take the sleigh and settle the reindeer.

"This is incredible," I breathed.

"They spent all the budget on this. That's why the kitchen staff are so bad," Gilbert muttered. He had insisted on sitting with the one noisy case on his lap in the sleigh, terrified of allowing his precious pots and pans out of his sight.

He clambered out of the sleigh awkwardly.

Claus Cottage was a hubbub of activity already by the time I arrived the next morning to say farewell to Nick.

Gilbert opened the large front door for me, his expression weary.

"Ready for the peace and quiet to return?" I asked.

"Santa knows I love all of the Clauses dearly, but I must be getting lazy in my old age. Not a moment goes by without someone needing a drink or a snack or a hot water bottle!"

"They are all capable of helping themselves, you know," I said, only realising my mistake after the words had left my lips.

"Oh! Miss Holly Wood, I see! I see! You think I'm the kind of elf who would allow the Claus family to help themselves, do you? Is that the kind of elf I am? I might as well just hang up my..."

"Good morning Holly, dear! Come on in! Gilbert, move aside, dear. It's below freezing out there," Mrs Claus appeared behind Gilbert and he obediently moved away and let me enter.

"I'll just go and check on the bacon," he mumbled, and disappeared towards the kitchen.

"Breakfast?" I asked.

"Oh, no, they've already had breakfast. Gilbert's insisting on making bacon cobs for the road!"

"Aren't you tempted to join them?" I asked.

Mrs Claus laughed. "I'm more than happy to stay home in the warm, Holly. Not to mention, there's so much to be doing here."

"I'm looking forward to helping with Mistletoe Matchmakers," I said. "Although I've not had much luck with love so I don't know how much help I can be with speed dating!"

Mrs Claus eyed me, a question unspoken on her tongue.

"I mean, of course, I didn't have much luck dating before... erm... before Nick," my cheeks flushed.

"So you're officially dating! That's wonderful news, Holly! I didn't like to pry but that's excellent news. I suppose the engagement will be the next step? How exciting!"

I shifted on my feet. "We haven't spoken about getting engaged."

"Well, of course not! It has to be a surprise, doesn't it. The man surprises the woman. Planning it all out wouldn't be very romantic, now would it?"

"The woman can propose too, you know?" Heidi's singsong voice came from behind us.

"Of course! I just mean, traditionally, it was the man. But sweet Heidi has a point. If you want to be engaged, Holly, go right ahead and propose! Don't wait around for Nick!"

I swallowed. The whole conversation was careering ahead like a sleigh on a patch of black ice and I was in the passenger seat, powerless to stop it.

"I'll give it some thought," I said. "Anyway, where is everyone?"

"Sir, shall I help?" The valet offered.

"Absolutely not. The items in here are worthless! Utterly worthless!"

"Dear, I think you mean priceless," Mrs Claus said with a wink towards the valet, who recognised her and became immediately flummoxed.

"Mrs Claus! It's an honour, an absolute honour to meet you again!"

Father Christmas placed his arm around her and cleared his throat.

"Father Christmas, great to have you back!" The valet said, as if greeting an old friend.

"Nick, are you watching? This is what it's like to have a wife more liked and admired than you. You should prepare for this, son."

I flushed at the mention of marriage, but Nick just grinned at me.

"Mum's quite the Mrs Claus to follow," he said to his dad, who gave a sage nod and looked across at me, held my gaze.

We all filed inside and the Claus family collapsed into various cozy chairs and settees. A huge log fire sat against one wall of the large living space, and tucked up against the far wall was a discreet bar, nestled at an angle so that the Claus family could have privacy from the bar staff.

I watched as Rascal headed straight across to the bar, where he was served by a tall, young man with mousy hair and a smattering of teenage acne across his pale face.

"This place is amazing," I gushed.

"It's not bad, huh? You know, Holly, we used to come out and ice fish in a little teepee, that's what all the camps were originally. But there was some concern that we should stay somewhere a little..."

"Warmer?" I asked Father Christmas.

"More up market. Rudolph forbid we might slum it a little," Heidi said with a smile.

"The people of Candy Cane Hollow put this family on such a pedestal, Holly. It's really very sweet of them," Mrs Claus said.

"Most of them put you on the pedestal and tolerate the rest of us, mum," Nick grinned.

"Guys. The bar's open. What's wrong with you all?" Rascal plopped down on a chair, a drink of amber liquid in each of his big, meaty hands. He downed one, winced, shook his head, then downed the second.

"Call us crazy but most of us can get through an hour-long sleigh ride without needing a drink right after," Clive exclaimed.

"You're crazy," Rascal said, then turned his attention to Norman, who was glancing around the room. "What's got into him?"

"You know what he's like here, always security conscious," Heidi shrugged. "Making sure the sleigh wasn't followed."

"Security conscious?" I asked. Maybe I had been right to tell Nick to be careful out at Camp Mackerel! But I'd meant because of the dangers of ice fishing, nothing else.

"You haven't told her?"

"Told me what?"

Nick groaned. "It's just a rumour..."

"It's a conspiracy theory! Everyone loves a conspiracy theory!"

"There are some valid reports coming out, Rascal, but trust you to say it's a conspiracy theory because they're by women not men," Heidi admonished.

Rascal looked at her seriously. "Sweetheart, I have no

interest in reading Bigfoot reports, whether they're by men or women."

"Bigfoot?! As in, like, the abominable snowman?! Is this a joke?" I exclaimed.

"We're not allowed to call him abominable, apparently. It hurts his feelings," Rascal said.

Nick pulled me away from the group and sat with me by the fire. "It's nothing to panic over. There have been some sightings out here, and a few of the smaller teepee camps have had food stolen, but it's nothing to worry about."

"You're telling me that Bigfoot is out here?" I asked, unable to believe that what I was hearing was true. But, the person speaking to me was the next Santa in training, so my perspective was probably a little off.

Nick squirmed a little at the question. "There are people who believe he is, sure. It's not something I believe. It's kind of, like, what's that sea creature thing up in Scotland?"

"The Loch Ness Monster?"

"That's it! Do you believe in that?"

"Well, I've never really given it much thought, but if you're asking me on the spot whether I believe there's a huge monster living in a Scottish lake... I'm going to say no."

"But some people believe it, right? And they say they've seen it? And there are even some photographs?"

I nodded. "I get it. You have people here who believe in Bigfoot, but he's not real."

"Oh, erm..."

"What?"

"He's real. Definitely real. Quite a nice guy to be honest, although he has a bit of a temper. But he's not here, that's the point."

"Drink?" A voice interrupted us before I could take in

the revelation that Bigfoot was, indeed, real and apparently a nice guy.

I looked up to see the teenager from behind the bar, a pad and pencil in his hands.

"Oh, hey Tomas. This is Holly," Nick introduced.

I rose to my feet and held out a hand, watched as Tomas clumsily rearranged the paper and pencil into the same hand and offered me his other to shake. He had a surprisingly firm grip and I tried not to wince.

"Nice to meet you. I've been wondering when Nick would bring a lady friend out here," Tomas said.

"You can't have been wondering that long, surely? You look young."

Tomas grinned. "Everyone says that. I'm 27. People see the spots and think I must still be sixteen."

"Oh, no, it's not that, you just have a youthful look," I spluttered as my cheeks grew red.

"Well, thanks. What do you think to this place?"

"It's incredible," I admitted.

Tomas beamed with pride as if he'd personally designed and built the place, and I wasn't about to assume he hadn't.

"Tomas is the caretaker for the place. He tends bar while we're here, and when we're not, he keeps the place humming along."

"Oh. Great!"

"It's harder than it sounds. Can you imagine how much time I spend cleaning those windows after every snow storm?"

I looked at the huge panes of glass and admitted that I could not imagine that.

"You stay out here alone?"

"Oh, no, that'd be lonely. There's a group of us."

"Bella's still here?" Nick asked.

"I believe so," Tomas said with a tight smile. "Anyway, what do you want for drinks?"

Nick cringed.

"I'll get a white wine, please," I ordered.

"My normal, please," Nick requested.

We both watched as Tomas moved on to ask everyone else for their own drink orders.

"He seems nice," I said.

"Yeah, he's always been a great asset to Camp Mackerel. Not many people want the job, staying out here for months at a time."

"I can't imagine it suiting many people," I said with a smile.

"It doesn't. But the ones who do like it, they tend to stay for years. We get students who pass through, too, work a summer or a year off and then go back to their regular life. And it's great for creatives; we have a few people who come for three months a year and spend their down time writing books or painting."

"Like a creative retreat with some housekeeping to do. It sounds pretty cool when you put it like that."

Our drinks arrived, delivered by a pretty young elf with long dark hair and smudged make-up around her eyes. Her cheeks were red and she didn't quite make eye contact with us.

"Hey, thanks Bella. Meet Holly," Nick introduced.

Bella looked up and offered a shy smile. "Hey. Hey Nick."

"Nice to meet you. Thanks for the drinks," I said.

"Sure, anytime. Enjoy your stay!" Bella said, and she was gone, moving back towards the bar with the empty drinks tray by her side.

"A quiet one," I said with a smile as I took a sip of the wine. Nick had ordered a cocoa and a dangerous amount of marshmallows balanced precariously on top of the cream foam.

"Very quiet. Again, not uncommon in a person who chooses to practically live out here. She's actually one of the fishing guides."

"She is?" I asked, surprised that someone with her youth had such a technical job. Not that I had any idea how technical it was to be a fishing guide, but it sounded very impressive to my novice ears.

Nick nodded. "She comes from a long line of ice fisher-elves. And the old guy over there with the beard? That's Salty. He's been here at Camp Mackerel the longest, I remember him from when I was a kid."

I looked over and saw a small, wrinkled man with a long white beard and big yellow fishing boots.

"He looks a character," I said with a smile.

Nick laughed. "Oh, he's that all right. He drives Gilbert madder than a cook who can't find any cranberry sauce. Salty's a little, erm, more relaxed about keeping things clean. They have some real humdingers!"

Even as we watched, Gilbert side-eyed Salty and then let out a flamboyant sigh and rose to his feet.

"Oh, Salty, my dear friend, you appear to have forgotten our little talk!" Gilbert crooned.

Salty looked at him and raised a single, crazed eyebrow.

"I know it's hard to remember, especially at your age, but we had a little heart to heart last year about how important it is to keep things clean. This is Camp Mackerel, remember, not the Rent-A-Hole out on Twilight Twig Express."

"It's ringing a bell with me, now, Gilbert, my old pal. Is that the talk where you told me if I ever wore my fishing boots inside again you'd stuff me like a turkey?"

Rascal spat out a good mouthful of what must have been his fourth glass of whisky and descended into laughter.

"I believe it went something like that, Salty, yes," Gilbert offered his most insincere smile.

"Well then. I guess you better get your baster ready," Salty said with a chuckle as he stomped across the old rug, mainly for show.

Gilbert watched, aghast, then turned to Mrs Claus. "You don't even use a baster to stuff a turkey! Does he know nothing about how a kitchen works?! It's a merry good thing that I brought my tools with me!"

5

After enjoying the welcome drinks, most of the group retreated upstairs to get changed into their fishing clothes.

Nick had offered me the chance to get out onto the ice with him, but I'd declined. I'd be happy to catch up on some time with Mrs Claus, and maybe even a little reading, and then see Nick later to hear all about his fun out there in the cold.

I sat in a comfy armchair and pulled my legs up underneath me. My one glass of wine had taken off the shock of the Bigfoot revelation, and I'd moved on to a hot cocoa, wrapping my hands around it to keep them warm.

A movement across the room caught me eye and I watched as Norman returned from upstairs and sat at a stool by the bar.

Tomas appeared, shook his head and retreated back into the kitchen.

I decided to go and chat to Norman, see if I could bond with him a little more and maybe even extend an offer to listen if he ever wanted to talk about his loss.

By the time I'd picked up my drink, Norman had got his phone out and was tapping away at it in a fairly urgent way. Not wanting to interrupt, I lowered myself back into the chair. I'd go over when he finished what he was doing.

The kitchen door pushed open and Bella appeared. As soon as she saw Norman at the bar, she beamed at him and her cheeks flushed. He looked up, said something, and she nodded and laughed. A tendril of her dark locks fell free from behind her ear and she wrapped it in her fingers, played with it.

I watched and smiled to myself. There was something so universal in her body language, in the eager way she fixed her gaze on him.

I must have been making my interest too obvious, because Bella glanced at me then, and the smile disappeared from her face. I offered an encouraging smile, then forced myself to look away and focus on my drink.

By the time I dared glance up again, Bella had gone from behind the bar, and Tomas was back in position, drying glasses with a blank expression on his face.

Norman rose from the bar, noticed me and offered a wave.

"Are you coming out on the ice?"

"Oh, no. I think this is close enough for me," I said with a grin.

"That's a shame. You don't know what you're missing."

I gave a nervous laugh. "Maybe next year."

Norman grinned at me. "You're planning on sticking around that long? We haven't scared you away?"

"Oh, well, I mean, a lot can change in..."

"Holly, relax. It's obvious that you and Nick are mad about each other," Norman said.

I cocked my head, surprised by his romantic side.

His cheeks flushed. "Wow. Well, I don't know where that came from. Don't tell my sister I just got all mushy for a second, okay?"

I grinned and held up my little finger. "Pinkie promise."

"Pinkie promise? What is that? You Londoners have some strange turns of phrase!" He teased.

There came a clattering down the wide staircase, and Norman and I both watched as Rascal came toppling down with a thud.

Before either of us could react, Tomas had sprinted across from the bar and kneeled beside Rascal, who was blinking and scowling as if the staircase had tricked him.

"Are you okay?" I asked as I dashed over.

"Someone must have left something on the stairs. I lost my footing somehow!"

Tomas draped Rascal's arm over his shoulder and pulled the larger man up on to his feet.

"How does that feel? Any pain?" Tomas asked.

Rascal shook his head, but winced.

"Should he be putting weight on his legs?" I asked.

Tomas shrugged. "He's either going to see how bad it is here, or out there. I'd prefer he does it here."

"Good point," I agreed.

Tomas gradually let go of his supportive hold on Rascal, and I watched as he gingerly trod around the room, his Mohawk dancing as he swayed unsteadily from side to side.

"It's kind of hard to tell how much is the walk of an injured man, and how much is the alcohol," Norman called from across the room.

Tomas shot him a look but said nothing.

"How do you feel?" I asked Rascal.

"Oh baubles, I forgot we have a lady doctor in the house!" Rascal grinned.

"You can just say doctor, you know, this isn't the 1970s," Heidi said as she appeared at the bottom of the staircase in the most adorable grey and black ski suit. She noticed the exaggerated gait of Rascal's walk and approached him. "Are you okay, uncle?"

"Sure, sure! I was just checking in with Holly here and seeing if she was ready to ditch Nick and hang her baubles on a more mature man," Rascal said with a wink.

Heidi imitated being sick.

I laughed. "You must be feeling okay if you're up to joking around."

"Who's joking?" Rascal asked.

"I hope you're behaving, Rascallion, dear," Mrs Claus said as she led the remaining family members down the stairs and into the room.

"You know me, Mrs C!"

"Exactly, that's why she's asking," Gilbert said. "Now, I've packed a few snacks for you mad fools who are braving the icy wilderness. You wouldn't get me out there for love nor mince pies, not even yours Mrs Claus!"

"That's nice, dear. You stay here with me and Holly. We're going to work on the plans for the Mistletoe Match-makers. And maybe have a game of Penguin Pairs!"

Gilbert humphed. "Well, it's alright for some. Penguin Pairs, indeed! I'd love to join in, Mrs Claus, but I'll be toiling in that kitchen for hours, I just know it. I can't imagine how much grease and dirt there'll be lurking in there. You know, I imagine I'll have to clean every single utensil before it meets the standards you're used to."

"Goodness, dear, that does sound like a lot of work," Mrs Claus said. When Gilbert wasn't looking, she shot me a wink. We all knew that the dramatic elf loved working and hated being without a job to do.

"Well, we'd better get going. There isn't much daylight out here and we want to have a few hours before heading back for dinner," Father Christmas' booming voice got everyone's attention.

"I'm excited!" Heidi exclaimed.

"Me too," Harry admitted.

Art stood at the back of the group, his book not in front of his face, but clutched tightly in his hand. I struggled to imagine the boy enjoying ice fishing, but couldn't imagine he got much of a choice with Rascal as his father.

"Let's get this show on the ice," Rascal said. There was still a slight gingerness when he put his left foot down on the ground, but he was clearly not going to let it stop him having a great time.

As everyone stomped into their boots, I found Nick and pulled him close.

"Promise you'll be careful?" I asked.

"Of course. I know what I'm doing. And we have the guides out there with us. I'll be back in a few hours. Don't worry. Try and have some fun here. And relax! You work so hard, try and enjoy this down time."

"Oh, I have every intention of doing that. I am switching off and getting into relaxation mode," I said with a smile.

Nick beamed at me. "Good. You deserve it, Holly. Oh, and by the way, they all love you."

I couldn't hide my smile. "Really?"

He nodded. "I knew they would, but I know you were nervous. And I get it. I'll be just as nervous when I meet your family."

I stopped in my tracks. My family. I hadn't even imagined August meeting Nick. Of course I wanted her to, but how could I explain that the man in my life was currently training to be Santa? I gulped.

"I mean, there's no rush. I wasn't asking... I..."

I cleared my throat and tried to think of words that would reassure him, but none came out.

"It's fine, really. If this is all moving too fast, just... maybe I'm rushing you? Wow, I'm such a klutz."

"No, Nick, I..."

"Nicholas?" Father Christmas' voice called out. In my focus on Nick, and panic about my sister, I hadn't even realised that the rest of the party had all left. Only Nick and I remained near the staircase, holding up the rest of the ice fishing party.

"Coming, dad," he called. He looked back at me, seemed to consider moving in for a kiss, but then doubted himself and left with a wave.

I watched as he closed the door behind him, and saw the sleighs move off through the huge window.

As soon as they were gone, I closed my eyes and groaned. I'd sent Nick off into the dangerous icy wilderness thinking I didn't feel the same way about him as he did about me.

What had I done?!

6

After spending a few hours working on the plans for Mistletoe Matchmakers with Mrs Claus, eating an elaborate lunch that Gilbert insisted was something he'd just knocked together in five minutes, and reading a chapter of my book, I grew restless and decided to go for a walk.

Camp Mackerel had extensive winter gardens, bordered with conifer trees and featuring incredible ice statues. I strolled around and took in the sights, and was giddy with excitement when I saw an arctic fox tucked underneath one of the trees, watching me warily.

I crouched down a few feet away from it and watched as it flicked its luscious tail, then stood up and slowly approached me.

"Oh, wow. Hey, baby!" I whispered.

The fox came closer, sniffed, then sauntered off towards another tree.

The magical moment was interrupted by my mobile phone ringing from within my pocket. My patients were being looked after by a colleague, but I'd told them to call me if they had any queries at all.

"Hello, Dr Wood speaking."

"Holly, dear! It's me! Nick's home," Mrs Claus' breathless tone informed me.

"Oh, that's great. He made good time! Thanks for letting me know," I said, as I watched the fox side-eye me, no doubt annoyed that I'd brought a phone call out to disturb the peace.

"I think you should head back."

"I'm just having a walk. I won't be too much longer," I said with an indulgent smile. Mrs Claus just couldn't get enough of seeing her son with a partner.

"Oh, no, of course. You're right!"

Something about her cheery tone was off and stopped me in my tracks. "Wait. Is everything okay?"

"Nick's fine, dear, I didn't mean to alarm you. You enjoy your walk!"

"I'll be back in a few minutes," I said, and ended the call before Mrs Claus could object.

I left the carefully maintained footpath and took a short cut across the deep pile of snow, knowing that my boots wouldn't protect my feet from the cold, and not caring.

There was something wrong.

I knew it.

Camp Mackerel was a hive of activity as soon as I arrived.

Gilbert opened the door but didn't quite meet my gaze. His normal dramatics were missing.

"I'll make cocoa," was all he said as he closed the door behind me and retreated to the kitchen.

I heard voices in the den area, all speaking over each other.

As I moved into the space, only Mrs Claus noticed, and she dashed across and swooped me up towards the bar before I could find a seat.

"Holly! You must be frozen from that walk! What you need is some hot soup!" She scolded as she manoeuvred me onto a bar stool.

"I'm fine!"

"Nonsense. Gilbert, dear, can you rustle something together for Holly? She's been outside in the cold."

Gilbert assessed me, then opened a fridge behind the bar and pulled out ingredients for a BLT without saying a word.

"What's happened? Something's wrong here," I said.

I thought I heard Gilbert try to hide a sniffle as he worked with his back to us.

"Well, yes, there is a slight issue, dear. But I'm sure it will be sorted."

"Holly?" Nick's voice came from behind me, his tone as smooth as caramel, his forehead etched with worry.

I moved to him and enveloped him in an embrace, glad to be close to him, whatever had happened.

"What's wrong?" I asked.

"Well, dear, it's just a little mix…"

"Mum, I'll explain," Nick said with a swallow that made his Adam's apple bob. "We've lost Norman. Bella too."

Before I knew it, I had laughed. I clamped my hand over my mouth in horror. "Lost them? What do you mean?"

"Out there, on the ice. We searched for them but couldn't find them."

"You mean they're…" I glanced out of the kitchen window at the thick falling of snow coming down. "They're still out there?"

Nick met my gaze and gave a short nod. I couldn't read

his expression and didn't want to panic him any more than he already was.

"Well, Bella's experienced, right? They'll both be fine, I'm sure. Maybe they just got a little disorientated."

Nick frowned. "That's the worry. That's a deadly mistake to make out there."

"You've called for help?" I asked.

"Wiggles is on his way over," Mrs Claus confirmed. The festive Chief Superintendent didn't strike me as a man who could track a lost soul over the ice, but he had surprised me in plenty of other ways in the time I'd known him.

"That's good. It's going to be fine, I'm sure," I said. "How's everyone doing?"

Nick shrugged. "Much as you'd expect really."

"Oh! Poor Heidi!" I exclaimed, thinking that she couldn't possibly lose her brother after losing their father. I wasn't insensitive enough to say that out loud, thankfully. "Can I see everyone?"

Nick led me into the main sitting area and I gave awkward smiles to each relative.

"He never did know his left from his right," Rascal said with a hearty laugh. I flinched at the past tense he used.

"We'll leave no slab of ice unturned until we find them," Father Christmas' voice boomed. The voice of reason. The voice of reassurance.

Heidi's eyes were swollen and red. She nodded, but said nothing.

***

The loud beats of Last Christmas alerted us to Wiggles' arrival before his fist beat a rhythm on the door.

I jumped up to let him in, pleased for the excuse to get out of the heavy atmosphere in the den for a moment.

"Holly," he beamed at me. "How are they all doing?"

"They're sadder than the children on the naughty list. Wiggles, I know I'm new here and no expert on ice fishing, but this is bad, right?"

"Oh, yes! Awful bad. Getting yourself lost out there on the ice is about as silly a thing as you could do."

"What will you do?" I asked. My stomach churned as I considered Norman out there, all alone.

Wiggles made a show of checking his watch. "We'll organise a search party, of course we will, even if it's probably already too... anyway! Enough of this chatter! Let's get in there and ask some questions!"

Already too... it was easy to guess how his sentence was going to end. I appreciated him stopping himself, but he wasn't saying anything I hadn't considered myself.

"Did they do the right thing leaving them?" I asked.

"Any ice fishing casualty is a terrible thing, Holly. But a whole family wiped out because they stuck around longer than they should? That would have been a tragedy. The Claus family have to survive. What could they have done, anyway? Split up to look for the pair of them? Followed after them so they got lost too? They had to come home and raise the alarm."

"Okay," I said, placated. "Well, come on in."

The chatter in the room died down as Wiggles moved across to the middle of the den. I followed behind him and took the seat next to Nick.

"Well, good evening," Wiggles said with a thin smile.

"We appreciate you coming out here," Father Christmas rose and shook the policeman's hand.

Wiggles removed his snow hat and spent a moment gazing respectfully at his shoes before pulling a pen and notebook from his pocket.

"Let's take it one step at a time. Who was the last person to see them?"

The Claus family looked around at each other but nobody seemed keen to answer.

"I'm thinking you followed the Ice Fishing Regulations, Rule 43B(A)?"

"Of course they did, dear!" Mrs Claus gushed.

"There are ice fishing regulations?" I whispered to Nick.

He nodded. "Because of how dangerous it can be. That rule states that nobody be out on the ice for any period of time alone."

"Makes sense," I said.

"I was his buddy," Rascal said. "We all paired up and I got the short straw."

"Okay. So talk me through what happened," Wiggles asked.

"We fished in pairs, as Rascal said. We all gathered for food at a set time. Gilbert had packed us some wonderful snacks. Norman headed off alone and that was the last we saw of him," Father Christmas explained.

"He headed off alone? None of you went with him?" Wiggles asked.

"We were eating. My fingers were near froze and I'd just sat down for some turkey curry," Rascal said.

"And your foot was hurting, dad," Harry added.

Rascal pulled a face. "I needed to eat."

"Rule 43B(A) is there for a reason," Wiggles muttered.

"How about Rule 12.2?" Rascal shouted, his face red.

"That's a fair point," Wiggles said. "Eat something warm every four hours, no excuses."

"Anyway, Rascal did go after him, just not immediately," Heidi said, her voice weak.

"You followed his tracks?" Wiggles asked.

Rascal shook his head. "The snow was coming down in Santa sacks. There were no tracks."

Wiggles let out a long exhale. "What did he have with him for provisions?"

Nick's voice cracked beside me. "He had nothing. He just upped and left."

"Why would he do that? He knows better! Should I be concerned that he's stepped out on some kind of suicide mission?"

I'd never seen Wiggles so frustrated. It was clear he had strong ideas about safety in the icy wilderness, and I couldn't blame him.

"I don't think so," Clive said. "We'd been chatting about his plans for the future. He seemed fine. Positively excited, for Norman, to be honest."

"He seemed okay to me," Nick agreed.

"He have any weapons on him?" Wiggles asked.

"Weapons?" Father Christmas asked.

Wiggles gave an awkward shrug. "I have to know what kind of situation I might be sending my officers into."

"Of course you do, dear. Norman's never had a gun," Mrs Claus said with a smile.

"He left his knives at the camp when he walked off," Rascal said.

"And how about the guide?"

"Bella was doing some inspections of the hole sites while we ate. She never came back," Nick explained.

"She didn't eat with you?" I asked.

Nick shook his head. "None of the guides do. It's their job to have the holes ready for us. If anything, they eat while we fish."

"The rest of the guides came back to camp okay?" Wiggles asked.

Father Christmas nodded.

Wiggles turned to look at the guides, who were seated by the door, each with stricken looks on their faces. I recognised Salty, and there were two others beside him.

"You guides followed Rule 43B(A)?"

The guides shifted in their seats but none of them answered.

"I asked you a question," Wiggles said.

"Look, we know the ice better than we know the backs of our hands. We save time by working alone," Salty said.

Wiggles rubbed his temple. "You led by example! You have to stay together!"

"Oh, for crackers sake! With respect, I don't see you out on the ice making sure a fishing trip is being organised properly, when the holes are filling in with fresh snow in less time than it takes for you to eat a mince pie. If we insist on working in pairs, things get dangerous out there pretty quick," Salty said with a glare.

"Looks like things have got pretty dangerous, alright. I'll deal with you all later. Now, you were at Camp Walrus?"

"It's our lucky spot," Clive exclaimed, then grimaced. "Well, it used to be."

"And we were following Rule 187. We all drilled down no more than a mile from the camp," Father Christmas confirmed.

"Okay. I'll get a search party assembled. One last thing - I'm guessing you've tried phoning them? No signal out there?"

"He left his phone at camp," Nick said.

Wiggles nodded, as if that was the answer he'd been expecting.

"Bella's phone is going straight to Polar voicemail."

"Oh! Before I forget. Do you have a photo of them? I'm

sure we all know what Norman looks like, but I should have one on the file."

"There'll be a photo of Bella in her HR folder. The manager's office is upstairs, dear," Mrs Claus said.

"You can take this," Heidi said. She reached into her bag and opened her purse to pull out a recent picture of her and Norman together. His arm was slung around her shoulder and the two of them were laughing. She gazed at the photo for a second, sniffed, then handed it out for Wiggles.

7

I was the first one up the next morning, which never happened at Claus Cottage. Gilbert considered it his elfly duty to be the first up, and the rest of the household were early risers too.

I was pleased that they were all managing something of a lie in, since nobody had slept well the night before. I'd laid awake most of the night, and had heard the staircase creak constantly as others ventured downstairs as sleep evaded them too.

As soon as the sun began to rise, I padded down the grand staircase and picked up the newspaper from the mat by the front door. In happier times, I'd no doubt have been amazed that someone had delivered a newspaper all the way out here at Camp Mackerel.

I moved across to the den area in a blur. The various mugs of cocoa that everyone had stayed up late drinking the night before had gone, magically swept away by Gilbert.

Curling up on one of the seats, I opened the newspaper and read the headline with a gasp.

A LOST CLAUS: NORMAN & NICK'S GRUDGE
REVEALED

How had the press become aware of Norman going
missing so quickly? And what grudge did they mean?

I continued reading.

*Norman Claus, 32, is missing feared dead following the
annual Claus Family Ice Fishing trip.*

*Claus, nephew of Father Christmas and second in line to the
title, failed to return from the first day's fishing on the exclusive
annual retreat with the rest of the Claus family.*

*Chief Superintendent Wiggles is understood to have launched
a search party, although it is clear that Claus could not survive
for long in the icy wilderness. Also missing is an ice fishing guide,
Bella Baubles.*

*The Claus Family's Ice Fishing trip has been a tradition for
many years, with the luxurious Camp Mackerel used as their
base.*

*While a Claus has never been lost on an Ice Fishing trip,
concerns have been raised about the safety of the pursuit for a
family with such important public duties.*

*Several lives have been lost while ice fishing over the years,
most notably the entire Humpback Missionary Collective Expedition team of 1982. While the team themselves were never found,
their expedition diaries were, and they feared that they were
being hunted by abominable snowmen.*

*Returning to Claus, his life has not been without tragedy
already. His father, Barry Claus, passed away and it is understood that he is not close to his mother.*

*While the Claus family are usually close knit, a source close
to them believes that there are tensions between Claus and his
cousin, Nick Claus, the current Santa-in-training.*

*"They fought often as children and following Barry's death,
Norman became more and more jealous about everything that*

Nick has - the happy home life, the stable career as Santa. Norman grew up visiting Claus Cottage and seeing what his life could have been. There has always been a tension between them. It was getting worse, not better, as they grew older. It's not easy to be part of the Claus family when you're not the main event."

This is true. Many junior Claus relatives find happiness by devoting themselves to things other than Christmas. Sid Claus PhD has a successful career in the pharmaceutical industry, and Benedict Claus was a literary agent before ill health forced him to take early retirement.

It seems that the key to happiness in the Claus family is the same as for the rest of us - to design a life we are happy with, and live on our own terms.

Will Norman ever get the chance to do this, or will his dreams forever be shattered - like the ice he was fishing on?

8

I put on socks, shoes, my chunky scarf, a woolly hat and a coat and quickly scurried outside to put the newspaper in the bin.

This wasn't easy and I looked quite the sight attempting to stomp through the knee-high snow without making any noise or being seen.

I finally reached the back of Camp Mackerel and found that the waste bins were taller than I was. How did anyone manage to get into the things?!

I found an ornamental garden table, climbed on to it, and managed to lift the bin lid and toss the newspaper inside, but the movement made the table wobble and fall to the ground, where it made no noise but caused the snow to explode like talcum powder all over my clothes and hair.

I grabbed on to the bin lid and managed to hold on, and hung there, swinging, for a few moments before I braved the short jump down for a landing not as soft as it looked.

I landed with a groan and had to giggle. There was probably not a career as a stunt double in my future.

I got to my feet, dusted myself down as best I could, and returned to the front of Camp Mackerel.

True, the article seemed more style than substance, but none of the Claus family would want to read it.

I was sure that it was difficult for members of the family who would never be Santa, but I couldn't see that reading a newspaper article about that would make any of them feel better.

I knew that Nick already felt awkward enough about the role he had been born to fulfil.

Pleased with my efforts to save the Claus family more heartache, I pushed open the door and realised that everyone had woken up in the few minutes I'd been gone. The smell of bacon came from the kitchen and voices filled the air.

"Hey! Everyone seen this newspaper article?" Rascal called as he returned from the bar with what appeared to be a Bloody Mary in his hand. He looked at me and did a double take. "Well, you look quite the sight."

"Just been out for a... erm... walk!" I said with a grin, but his interest had already moved on.

"Sons! You seen this rubbish?" Rascal continued, holding his enormous phone up. Harry gamely took the phone from his father and scrolled down the article. The rest of the family had gathered in the hallway.

I cringed as Harry read aloud the exact article that I'd just risked hypothermia to dispose of!

"They think Nick killed Norman," Harry said with a shrug, after reading the whole article aloud.

Rascal laughed. "You've misread it, son, it says nothing like that."

Harry raised a ginger eyebrow. "They're saying it without saying it. They don't want to be sued."

"Sued by who? By us, dear? We never sue anyone! We're impartial... like the Queen!" Mrs Claus said with a firm nod of her head.

"It's the best way to be. Once you start the process of suing the press every time they lie, it's easy for people to know which articles are true. Better to never have a public opinion," Harry said.

"Thank you, dear," Mrs Claus planted a kiss on his cheek then noticed me. "Holly, you look frozen!"

"Goodness gumdrops! I'll fetch blankets!" Gilbert exclaimed, and raced up the staircase.

"I'm fine," I said with a self-conscious smile, as everyone was now looking me up and down and wondering why on earth I'd been out into the cold and got so wet. Especially with Norman and Bella missing. It must have looked very insensitive of me.

"Let me see that article!" Clive asked, bursting through the crowd of people to snatch Rascal's phone from him.

"What's wrong with you people? Am I the only one who stays up to date with the news?" Rascal asked, moving his phone out of Clive's reach.

"It's all bad news, anyway," Clive said with a sniff.

Rascal turned off his phone and pushed it back in his pocket. "There are some saucy pictures on my phone that you're too young to see, Clive. Anyway, Harry's read it for you. The press think Nick killed Norman."

"That's not what it..." I began, then stopped myself.

"Harry's at Cambridge, let's remember. Studying law. If that's what he says it says, then it says what he says," Rascal said.

We all took a moment to untangle that tongue teaser, and then my eyes met Nick's across the hallway.

"It's fine," Nick said. "We all know nobody's been killed.

The newspapers are always going to jump to the most controversial conclusions. Norman's not even dead! He'll have found Bella and they'll be sheltering somewhere. They'll wander back over here with a story to tell and a demand for mince pies."

"Good point, Nick. I'd better bake more. Pop and turn the oven on for me, dear?"

Nick smiled at his mum, then he turned and headed into the kitchen.

Mrs Claus waited until he had gone, then lowered her voice. "Now, stop this nonsense. I know we're all worried, but Nick has no grudge against poor Norman!"

Tomas efficiently arrived with fresh cocoa for everyone, much to Gilbert's annoyance.

"You know, it's probably better that I make the drinks. I know how everyone likes them," Gilbert said with a simpering sweet smile.

Tomas shrugged. "It's cocoa. There's really no way to make bad cocoa."

Gilbert guffawed. "Oh, you'd be surprised."

"Mrs Claus, I just wanted to express my condolences. I can imagine how worrying this must be for you all. Please let me know if I can help at all," Tomas said as he placed a mug of cocoa in front of the family matriarch.

Mrs Claus reached for the young man's hand and gave it a squeeze. "Thank you Tomas, that's awfully kind of you. Norman and Bella will be back here in no time. You'll see."

"Come on, guys. Let's be honest with ourselves. They've been out there almost 24 hours now. Alone in the snow. Norman ain't coming back, and I for one am glad he's gone," Rascal said.

"Rascallion Claus, take that back," Father Christmas ordered. He stood taller, wider, grander than everyone else, and I wondered whether he had always had such an impressive presence or whether it came with the role.

"That boy's been a leech attached to this family. It's not right, to carry the Claus name and be such a good-for-nothing. In fact, there's another one of them coming up through the ranks and I can't believe I fathered him."

I glanced at Harry, who remained impassive apart from a slight tremble to his bottom lip.

"I'm talking about Art, and nobody worry about his feelings being hurt. He's still in bed, of course. If there hadn't been a DNA test, I wouldn't believe that boy was mine," Rascal said, on a roll.

"That's enough," Father Christmas said.

Rascal rolled his eyes and pushed through the crowd. "Is breakfast ready, or what? Do I need to come in and make it myself?"

He pushed through to the kitchen and let out a horrid cackle, a laugh that could only mean that something bad had happened.

"Oh, this is interesting!" He shouted.

The crowd moved as one through into the kitchen, where Nick sat in a haggard position up against the countertops. The look on his face was one of terror, and it took me a moment to realise why. There, between his thighs, was a huge icicle that seemed to have impaled him in place.

"Oh my! Are you hurt?" I asked as I rushed to his side.

"No, no, I'm fine," he reassured me as I planted a kiss on his forehead and took his hand in mine.

Rascal let out a whistle. "It's gone right through your trousers! Wow, an inch higher..."

Nick winced. "Don't."

"What happened?" Harry asked.

"I just... it was... I opened the door and..." Nick struggled to explain.

"It was boobytrapped," I said. "Someone tried to kill you."

"Nonsense! This girl has quite the imagination, Nick. Maybe lay off the cocoa before bed, hey, Holly? This is Candy Cane Hollow - icicles are falling all the time," Rascal spluttered.

"Not normally inside kitchens, dear," Mrs Claus said.

Gilbert appeared at her side from the hallway, a stash of blankets in his arms. "Especially not my kitchen!"

"This isn't your kitchen," Tomas said.

Gilbert rolled his eyes. "While I'm here, it's my kitchen. I spent all yesterday sprucing this place up, and boy it needed it! You think an icicle of this size could just be left to grow inside this space while I'm here? Do I look like the kind of elf who wouldn't spot it? Do you think I didn't include the ceiling when I cleaned yesterday? Why, I've got half a mind to just hang up my..."

"Okay, elf. That's enough out of you. You're enough to give a man tinnitus," Rascal said.

We all worked together to remove the icicle, then I helped Nick into the den, where he lay down on a settee and I gradually applied layers of blankets to help his skin warm back up.

"Are you really okay?" I asked.

Nick stared at me, his eyes darting about as if he wasn't entirely convinced he was safe.

"I'm okay Holly, but, do you really think someone tried to kill me?"

I nodded. "Like Gilbert says, there's no way a huge icicle like that would just be left above the door."

"But how would anyone know I'd be the next to walk in there?"

"I don't know," I admitted.

"Oh no."

"What?"

"You don't think it's linked, do you? This and Norman going missing?"

The idea had already occurred to me. "It would be a pretty big coincidence if they weren't linked."

Nick buried his head in his hands. "I can't believe this is happening. If we're right, this means that someone in this house is... is a homicidal maniac!"

"Let's not get carried away just yet. You need to relax, you've had a real fright and some exposure to the cold. Let's just see what happens, yeah? Norman and Bella could still turn up safe and this could all be explained innocently."

"Yeah, you're right," Nick said.

I squeezed his hand and gave what I hoped was a reassuring smile. As much as I didn't want Nick to panic, I had to admit that the chances were that he was right, and one of the Claus family was a homicidal maniac.

Wiggles knocked at the door without the normal *Last Christmas* playing out to warn us of his arrival, and that seemed a good indication that he was bringing bad news.

I'd just checked on Nick and was in the hall on my way to fetch him some more tablets and a glass of water, so I answered the door as I passed.

"Can I come in?" He asked, a sombre note to his voice.

I nodded and brought him in to the den, where everyone had gathered for mid-morning cocoa.

"You have news, Wiggles?" Father Christmas asked.

"I do. I came straight out. The team, they erm, they found a body."

"Norman?" Heidi asked, with a squeak.

"I mean, the waters are unforgiving. It's not easy to say for sure, but it's looking like it's Bella. We're as sure as we can be," Wiggles confirmed. "I'm sorry."

"Goodness gumdrops," Mrs Claus pulled Heidi into her bosom and the two began to cry.

"She was in the water?" Father Christmas asked. His own voice wobbled as he spoke.

Wiggles nodded. "She was. Only 100 feet from Camp Walrus, but you all know how easy it is to lose your sense of direction out there."

"I said that Norman never knew his left from his right, turns out neither did Bella!" Rascal exclaimed.

"She was a good guide. This should never have happened," Clive said.

"Oh, Tomas. Were you close to Bella?" Mrs Claus asked as Tomas collected the empty mugs.

The young man let out a long breath. "We were colleagues. I can't help thinking it's such a waste of a young life."

"Anyone can get into trouble on the ice," Harry said with a regretful shrug.

"But what about Norman?" Clive persisted.

"Clearly Norman, yes," Heidi snapped.

"Heidi, dear?" Mrs Claus gave her shoulders a squeeze.

Heidi closed her eyes. "If Bella hasn't made it, what chance does Norman have?

"Oh, Hei, I'm sorry. I just can't believe it," Clive gushed.

Heidi eyed him but said nothing.

"Was it a fishing hole that Bella fell through?" I asked.

"I'm afraid so. We'll investigate that. The hole should have been secured."

"Secured?" I asked.

"Rule 1 - never leave an open hole. Or we'd have ice fishing crews falling into holes all the time. At the end of the trip, each crew has to secure their holes. Apparently, another crew didn't do that because this hole wasn't a Claus hole."

"That's awful," I murmured.

"Any idea who the other crew were? They should be investigated," Harry asked, ever the law student.

Wiggles let out a whistle. "I don't fancy our chances of ever finding that out. You all know that nobody owns the ice. It could be anyone. Although, it's strange how close it was to Camp Walrus."

"Why?" I asked.

"Camp Walrus is only used by the Claus family," Father Christmas explained. "While nobody owns the ice, people do own the camps. Some of them are hotels, some are rented out by the night, and others are for private use only."

"But anyone could be out on the ice and just wander close to Camp Walrus?" I asked.

Wiggles seemed affronted by the idea. "Not if they respect Rule 187."

"That's basically to not venture more than a mile from your camp, right?"

Wiggles grinned. "You learn quick. Sure is."

"Do you think people follow all of those rules? It seems like there's a lot of them to remember."

Wiggles gazed at me as if I was speaking in another language. "What do you mean? Of course people follow the rules."

"Most of them are pretty obvious. Things you'd do even if you hadn't read the handbook," Nick explained.

"Who hasn't read the handbook? Annual re-reading of the handbook is a rule in itself! Rule 87B!"

"I've read it, of course I have," Nick gave a guilty chuckle.

"Okay, so, this is a really tragic case of someone not staying close enough to their own camp and not securing a hole. I wonder if a fishing crew went out to Camp Walrus to try to get close to the Claus family. Curiosity, perhaps."

"Well they wouldn't have been trying to get to the camp itself. That place is a dump," Heidi said.

"Camp Walrus is the oldest camp out there, it's not meant to be a luxury hotel. Some of these no-good turkey-eaters have forgotten how to rough it," Rascal said with a wink.

"That's not true, Rascal. I know how to slum it. I mean, I manage here, and there's only one swimming pool in the whole building," Heidi said. It was impossible to tell whether she was being sarcastic or not.

"There's only one swimming pool in the whole building!" Rascal repeated in an imitation of Heidi's voice. "You sound like my ex-wife."

"Which one?" Harry quipped.

Rascal batted his hand at his youngest son. "All of them. They were all trouble."

Wiggles cleared his throat. "Well, I erm... I'm sorry for your loss. We'll obviously continue searching for Norman."

"Thank you. And please, thank your search team. Nobody wants this to be the result of a call out," Father Christmas said.

"Of course. Do you all need anything else from me?" Wiggles asked as he placed his hat back on his head.

"I suppose we'll need to inform the family. Do you know who the next of kin is?" Father Christmas asked.

"You leave that with us."

"Thank you."

"I'll show you out," I said.

I escorted Wiggles outside and stood next to him by his car. Wiggles looked at me. "What's going on? You have something on your mind?"

"Someone attacked Nick. He was impaled by an icicle. It

missed his skin by a centimetre. Literally, it went right through his clothes and pinned him to the floor."

Wiggles' eyes became wide saucers. "When was this?"

"This morning."

"Here?"

I nodded. "In the kitchen."

Wiggles glanced around the side of Camp Mackerel.

"Is there a back door?"

I nodded, and led him around to the door that went straight into the kitchen. He pushed the door open and I followed quickly behind him, relieved that Gilbert had gone off into town to get groceries. He was precious about who stepped foot in his kitchen, even if it was a kitchen only temporarily under his control.

Wiggles surveyed the scene.

"What are you looking for?"

"Clues," he said. "Any sign of forced entry?"

"None, but the back door's always left open, so that doesn't mean much."

Wiggles nodded. "The whole of Candy Cane Hollow is the same. It seems like a good idea until... well, until it doesn't. You didn't notice anyone hanging around?"

"No, I didn't see anything strange at all."

"I'm guessing that elf of yours keeps a tidy kitchen. No chance of it being some kind of accident?"

"You mean could the icicle have been growing inside the house and just randomly snapped off and impaled Nick?"

Wiggles met my gaze. "I've seen it before in some, let's say, less well maintained homes."

"Well, that told me. Wow. Erm, no, Gilbert would never let that happen here. The first thing he did when we arrived was a full kitchen clean."

"I thought that would be the case."

"What do you think? I didn't want to panic Nick but it's bad, right?"

"It's worse than bad, Holly. Norman Claus is an experienced ice fisher. Bella Baubles even more so. Do I believe she just went off and fell into a hole? No way. That's no more likely than Nick's incident being an accident."

"What are you saying?"

Wiggles gazed right at me. "I'm telling you to be careful. Let's not let anyone know we're on to them, but we've got a homicidal maniac on our hands."

10

W iggles returned to the den and cleared his throat.

"Oh, hello again, dear! I thought you'd left already," Mrs Claus greeted him with a smile.

"I've got some difficult news," Wiggles said.

"Even more difficult than my brother probably being dead?" Heidi asked with a poker face.

"This is going to add to that, I'm afraid."

"Well, spit it out," Rascal called.

"Rascallion!" Mrs Claus scolded.

"He's as bad as that kitchen elf who can't stop nattering about nonsense," Rascal said, but he did at least lower his voice a fraction.

"I have reason to believe that more of you may be in danger. I could be overreacting, but I have to be cautious. I have no choice but to place you all under protective custody here at Camp Mackerel."

"What do you mean, dear?" Mrs Claus gazed at him blankly.

"He means that beautiful Bella was killed," Rascal exclaimed.

"That's nonsense, and you can just call a woman by her name without referring to her looks," Heidi objected.

"It's a possibility we have to consider," Wiggles said.

"No, no, you're right. You do have to consider it. But what makes you think anyone else is in danger?" Father Christmas asked.

"I'm not able to disclose that, sir."

Father Christmas considered that for a moment, then gave a nod. "I understand. Just what exactly are you proposing this protective custody involves?"

"He's putting us under house arrest, basically," Harry said, grateful for another chance to show off his legal knowledge.

"Not exactly. I'm going to assign some officers to stay here and look after you all. I can't force you to stay here, but I can only offer protection here. Resources are stretched, you'll understand, and we can't have an officer assigned to follow each of you around. So I would ask that you all stay here, and you'll be safe."

"Goodness gumdrops! How lucky we are to have such a pro-active police force. Wiggles, thank you for this."

"My pleasure, Mrs C," Wiggles said with the hint of a smile.

"Are you sure this is necessary?" Nick asked.

"Well..."

"It's just, there's so much to do to prepare for Christmas. We don't have any time to lose."

"Trust me, the last thing I want is to disrupt Christmas," Wiggles agreed.

Heidi let out a snicker. "That's funny, I'd have imagined

the last thing you'd have wanted would be another dead person on your hands."

"Of course, that's what I meant, of course I..." Wiggles gabbled on.

"Lay off him, Hi," Nick said with an awkward grimace. He hated any kind of confrontation, so his words were unusual, and everyone stopped and looked at him.

"I'm sorry. It's how I cope. I make fun of things. I'm sorry, Wiggles," Heidi offered.

Wiggles' cheeks flushed. "That's no problem. You've been through a lot."

"How long do you think this might last?" Father Christmas asked.

Wiggles glanced at his watch, as if that held the answer. "Not long, I hope. Just until we catch the k-, until we get this all resolved."

"Okay, well, we'll be here," I said.

11

With the whole Claus clan under effective house arrest, Gilbert was feeling the pressure. He zapped around the house in a blur, topping up drinks, offering snacks and panicking about how far the food in the camp would stretch.

"I'm sure the police will fetch provisions if we need more," I said.

Gilbert's mouth fell open. "The police will fetch provisions? Is that what you just said? Do you think Tweedle-dee and Tweedle-dum out there know how to shop for a baked ricotta and walnut risotto? Do you think they know the difference between arborio and egg fried when buying rice?"

"Well, I..."

"No, you're right. Everything I do here is soooooo easy, and soooooo replaceable! If that's what you think, I should just hang up my apron strings and be done!"

"Gilbert?" Father Christmas' booming voice came as he joined us in the kitchen.

"Right here! What can I get you?" Gilbert snapped to

attention. He doted on the whole family, but Father Christmas had a certain gravitas that couldn't be ignored.

"There's a young police officer at the door. She wants a shopping list. I figured I'd be useless at that kind of job. Would you mind?"

"Gilbert's already been out for supplies today," I said.

Gilbert's chest puffed out and he held his head high. "I'll do that right away. Better to have too much than not enough! I will not have my kitchen leaving anyone hungry!"

Father Christmas chuckled as Gilbert practically skipped off towards the kitchen. He took a moment to glower at Tomas, who insisted on maintaining his position behind the bar.

"How are you doing, Holly?"

I shrugged. "I've just rung Belinda and told her I might be back at work a bit later than I anticipated. She's going to warn my patients. Hopefully they'll understand."

"I'm sure they will. A police order isn't something to ignore. And I am pleased you're not trying to ignore it. I wouldn't want anything bad to happen to you. Gosh, we all know that Nick has struggled to find someone he has a real connection with. It's not easy being a Claus."

"Especially at the moment," I said.

Father Christmas' bushy grey eyebrows furrowed.

"Did you see anything out there?" I asked.

Father Christmas let out a sigh. "Here's one thing about the Claus family, Holly. The whole world imagines us to be magical beings, living in this constant winter wonderland and making children's dreams come true. And we are like that a lot, of course. But we're also a family. Sometimes we bicker. Sometimes we have bad moods, or bad days, but we can't show those to other people."

"That must be tough," I said.

"I hear you're quite the amateur sleuth," Father Christmas said.

"Well, I don't know about that."

"I'd like to ask you not to do that this time, Holly," his voice was stern, and I found that I couldn't quite meet his gaze.

"You would?" I managed to squeak.

The kitchen door opened and Gilbert burst across the room, still looking like the elf who ruled the roost. "Boy, it's a good job you didn't try to sort that one out. Would you believe that officer didn't know what a poinsettia was? I need to talk to Wiggles about his vetting processes!"

Only Gilbert could be ordering poinsettias at such a time. I flashed him a grin, keen to get away from my awkward conversation with Father Christmas.

"Well, I'd better go and, erm... powder my nose," I said, and backed out of the room before anyone could object.

The hallway was empty and I took a seat on the bottom step of the staircase. My mind was racing.

Why would Father Christmas warn me away from trying to investigate?

12

I tapped on the bedroom door and then walked in.

Nick was still resting his leg and he had been flicking through a toy catalogue, which he closed and placed beside him on the bed.

"Looking for gift ideas?" I teased.

He laughed. "It's important that I stay on top of the trends. There are so many new toys coming out nowadays. You know what I just found? Fish for Floaters! It's a fishing game, except instead of catching fish, you're trying to catch poops. Poops! Can you believe it? I mean, not real ones, that would be really gross."

I leaned in and planted a kiss on his forehead. "You're adorable. Even in your own sick bed while your cousin is missing, you're doing your homework."

"I'm a workaholic, I guess. I don't want to let my dad down."

I reached over and squeezed his hand. "I'm sure you could never do that."

"Anyway... out with it. I know you didn't climb all the way up that staircase just to check on me."

I considered protesting my innocence, but time was of the essence.

"I know you're going to be investigating. You don't have to pretend with me. You want to grill me?"

I grinned. "I was thinking I'd play good cop with you, since you're so cute."

"Oh! You think I'm cute, do you?"

"Maybe a little," I said as my cheeks flushed.

"This is an interrogation technique, right? Flatter me so my defences are down. Go on then, let's get this over with."

"The newspaper article... it said there was a grudge between you and Norman..." I stumbled over my words, not knowing how to broach the subject without causing Nick more upset.

"Your first question is whether I hurt him?"

"What?! No! Of course not!"

Nick laughed. "Holly, I'm teasing you. I know you'd never ask that. Just for the record, though, I didn't hurt him. Or Bella."

"So... the article isn't true?"

Nick frowned. "Honestly, I'd guess a lot of it was true. I'm the future FC, that's a lot for people to deal with. Norman's never found his passion in life. Maybe he did wish he'd been born in my position. And maybe that did make things awkward between us. I don't know."

"But there weren't any big disagreements between you two?"

Nick shook his head. "Not really. We fell out as kids, but that was all. Just regular family things. Then we grew apart, but we've never been hostile towards each other."

"Okay. That makes sense. If there was any jealousy, it might have caused Norman to drift away from you. Did you spend much time with him out on the ice?"

"Not really. I was partnered with Art."

"And then you went back to Camp Walrus. What happened then?"

"Rascal was limping, I noticed that. He seemed like he was in pain. Bella offered to look at his foot, but he refused. He wasn't exactly polite about it. So she and the other guides went off to make sure the holes were okay, and we got stuck into our food. Norman jumped up and left, and we all just kind of looked at each other, waited for Rascal to go with him."

"And he didn't?"

"He said that Norman probably needed the toilet again, which didn't make a lot of sense because Camp Walrus is basic but it does have a toilet. Then after a couple of minutes, dad got up to go after Norman, and Rascal went instead."

"Your dad was going to go after Norman?"

Nick nodded. "It was kind of clear that Rascal wasn't going to, and someone had to."

"How long was Rascal out there?"

"Only a couple of minutes."

"I hate to ask this, but long enough to do something bad?"

"Like hurt Norman?"

I nodded.

"I guess, but why would he?"

"They don't seem to like each other, Nick."

"But they're family. Family tolerate each other at least, right? And those two? They see each other once or twice a year and then get on with their own lives. It makes no sense."

"None of this makes sense, but we've got Norman missing and you injured. That can't be coincidence.

Someone is trying to hurt the Claus family. I'm thinking, could it be someone trying to get closer to being Santa?"

The colour drained from Nick's face as he realised what I was implying. "You think one of the family hurt Norman, and tried to hurt me?"

"I don't see another explanation."

"That's terrifying."

"Nick, if you and Norman both died, who would be the next Santa?"

Nick cringed. "Heidi."

I considered that for a moment, the hint of a clue returning to me.

"What?" Nick asked.

"Didn't it strike you as odd that Heidi had a photo of Norman in her purse to give to Wiggles? They're not that close, but she had the picture right there."

"Almost as if she knew one would be needed," Nick finished my thought process.

"I need to speak to her," I said.

"No, Holly. You need to be careful. Maybe you should leave this one to the police. Wiggles will get it all cleared up."

"Maybe. He's a good officer, I don't doubt that. But I can't just sit here and do nothing. Someone tried to kill you, Nick. They might try again."

Nick gave a nervous chuckle. "Gee, I love our uplifting chats."

"I'm serious. You need to be careful. You shouldn't be up here alone. I'm going to ask your mum to sit with you."

"You mean she's not on your suspect list?" Nick joked.

I burst into laughter and it felt so good to giggle after thinking such dark thoughts. "Thanks, I needed that."

"Is that everything?"

"I guess. I just feel sorry for Bella. I feel like she's somehow got wrapped up in this thing that's all about the Claus family."

13

M rs Claus was only too eager to agree to sit with Nick and not let him out of her sight.

I swallowed the guilt over the fact that I could be putting her in danger, returned to the den, and headed straight to the bar.

Tomas greeted me with a professional smile.

"I'll get a white wine, please," I said.

"Coming right up," he said and busied himself with pouring out the measure.

"How are you doing? I know that Bella was a friend of yours," I said.

Tomas grimaced and handed my drink to me. "I don't want to speak ill of the dead, but we were just colleagues."

"Oh, well, my mistake. Still, it can't be nice to lose a work colleague. I'm sorry for your loss."

There came a vibration from the bar counter and I saw as a mobile phone rang out. Tomas reached for it. "I have to get this."

"Oh, sure!" I said. I spun on the bar stool so that I was

facing the rest of the room. It would be good to sit back and observe the others, Heidi in particular.

I was intimidated by her a little, and unsure how to start the conversation with her. I could hardly come out and ask if she'd done something awful to her brother so that she could become the next Claus. Would she be the first female FC? As much as I didn't want to admit it, I could see that being the kind of thing that Heidi might be tempted to kill for.

Ugh. I shook my head. No, I had to speak to her and let her explain. Not decide she was guilty before even asking her a question.

"Yes, this is him. Yes, I've heard. Thank you. Oh, really? Well, a little surprised. No, no, of course. What do you need?" Tomas said, before taking the phone into the kitchen.

Heidi turned and looked in my direction and gave me a grin. A grin far too big and wide for a woman whose brother was still missing out on the ice.

To my horror and delight, she picked up her mug of cocoa and came right across to join me at the bar. Whether I was ready or not, it was time to talk to her.

"Hey, Holly! I'm not interrupting your peace and quiet, am I?"

"No! No way! I just ordered myself a drink," I picked up my wine glass and swilled it around a little.

"Good for you. I don't drink alcohol."

"Let me guess, you think it weakens our defences and makes us easier prey for the patriarchy?" I asked.

Heidi cocked her head, looked at me and then cackled. "I like that! That's good! But nope. It just sets off migraines."

"Oh, that's too bad. Have you had a neurology referral for them?"

Heidi shook her head.

"You should think about asking for one, to get everything checked out," I said.

Heidi smiled at me. "Thank you. It's handy having a doctor in the family!"

"Even just a GP?" I couldn't resist asking.

Heidi covered her open mouth with her hand. "I really hoped you'd forgotten about that. I get a bit too intense at times. I'm sorry. It's all this studying. My grades are all based on me making my point clearly and backing it up, there's no room for doubt. I guess I forget to switch back to human mode sometimes."

"It's fine," I said, eager to connect with the more human side of Heidi.

"Honestly, I think being a GP is awesome. I can't imagine how hard medical school must have been."

"Yeah, it was a slog at times. But you know about that, right? Being a Claus can't always be easy."

"Surrounded by all of these men? Are you kidding me!"

I decided the moment was right and reached for Heidi's hand, gave it a squeeze. "You must be so worried about Norman."

"Oh, no. It's pretty obvious at this point that he's not survived. Whatever happened, he's out of his misery now."

I gazed at her, stunned.

"Did that sound heartless? I just mean, there's no way he could have survived out there. He was okay at ice fishing, but ice survival is different. If Bella's dead, there's no way he isn't. I'd rather accept that and start the grieving process."

"It's strange how both of them got lost out there," I said.

Heidi shrugged. "Not really. She'd have been keeping a special eye out for him. If she saw him stomping off in a bad mood, she would have gone after him."

"Because she was a guide?" I asked, thinking that the ice guide job sounded ridiculously dangerous and not at all something to add to my future career goals.

Heidi gave a sad smile, glanced around us and lowered her voice. "Did you see the way she looked at him? She had a huge crush on him."

I thought back to how she had acted with him at the bar. "Well, that makes sense. The Clauses are a handsome family."

I cringed as I heard myself say handsome, and waited for a telling off for choosing such a masculine word.

Instead, Heidi smiled. "We are, aren't we?"

I laughed, relieved, and then we both grew quiet. "What do you think happened out there?"

"If I had to guess, I'd say that Norman went off and got himself into danger, and Bella noticed and went after him."

"But why would he go off into danger?"

Heidi shrugged. "I think he had something on his mind. He'd seemed distracted ever since we arrived here."

"You don't know what that could have been?"

"I wish I did. We just weren't close enough to talk to each other like that. I have a lot of regrets, Holly. I guess I thought that I'd had my share of grief, you know, with losing dad. I never thought I'd lose Norman too."

"It's awful," I said.

"I think if I'm honest, I imagined we'd have the whole of our lives to become closer to each other. It was a project for another day, you know, like clearing out my wardrobe or organising my digital photos. And now it's too late."

"Maybe not. He could still be found. You might get another chance," I said.

Heidi shook her head. "He's gone, there's no point in pretending otherwise."

She took a last sip of her cocoa, set the mug down, and gave my hand a squeeze, then got up and left.

I watched her go and felt the unease in my stomach.

I liked Heidi more after our chat than I had before. But I was also more certain that she was a murderer than I had been.

"Oh, Heidi, what aren't you telling me? How can you be so sure that Norman's dead?" I muttered.

"Did you say something, ma'am?" Tomas asked as he returned to the bar.

I turned and shook my head, apologised, and decided to get some fresh air.

14

Rascal was in the garden. True to his name, he had decided that staying in Camp Mackerel extended to the outer perimeter of the property's outside land.

I followed in his footprints - literally - and attempted to look casual as I caught up with him.

He was enjoying a secret cigarette, which he hastily put out as soon as he saw me approaching.

"Holly! Come out to join the rebel alliance, have you? They can take our freedom but they can never take our, erm, garden?"

I laughed. "I needed some fresh air."

"I don't blame you. I needed to get away from that lot and I'm related to them."

"Do you really not get along with your family, or is it a joke?"

Rascal considered the question. "I get along with the family just as well as I want to. Why? What's it to you?"

"I figured I might be able to help you out," I said.

"You did, now? Unless you're ditching Nick and coming out here for my number, I doubt it."

I laughed. "You know you're going to be the prime suspect, right?"

He guffawed but I saw his shoulders tense inside his heavy coat.

"You've been pretty open about your dislike of Norman, even just in the time I've known you. When the police come around and start asking questions, they'll think you killed him."

Rascal recovered his swagger and shrugged. He raised his eyebrows at me suggestively. "Maybe I did."

I swallowed my doubts.

I was standing outside, far enough away from Camp Mackerel for nobody to hear my screams, with the main murder suspect. Nick would definitely not approve.

But something told me there was more to this situation than the obvious answer.

"I don't think you killed anyone," I said. I looked out into the distance, just as Rascal was doing.

"Well, sweet cheeks, if I've got you on side, I'll be able to get the police on side too. I'll request a lady officer and she'll take one look at this face and tick me off the list. Probably invite me over for a steak dinner while she's at it. I've never dated a cop, come to think of it."

"It's going to be Wiggles himself who questions you all, and he's going to hear some things that will make him want to lock you away in Candy Cane Custody."

"Alright, I'll play along. Just how do you think you can help me?"

"I've solved a few cases before," I kept my voice neutral, not wanting to boast about the strange sideline I'd found myself involved in.

Rascal turned to face me and raised an eyebrow. "You, lady, are getting more interesting by the minute. You sure it's Nick you're into?"

I rolled my eyes and laughed. "Are you going to let me help you?"

"What exactly would it involve?" He asked, wary of committing.

"Just let me ask you some questions."

"Oh, you want to get to know Rascal better. Of course you do. This whole investigation thing is a ruse so you can spend some alone time with me! Well, sure thing. Let's go somewhere a little more cosy and we can talk."

I nodded, and Rascal led me further away from Camp Mackerel, right out to the very ends of the land, where a small log cabin stood.

Rascal pushed the door open and switched on the light.

Inside were a couple of reading chairs, a coffee table, a pair of binoculars and a telescope. A small table had a makeshift drinks station set up on it; a sink, kettle, three cups, jars of coffee, tea and sugar.

"What is this place?" I asked as I took a seat.

To my surprise, Rascal sauntered across to the table, and filled the kettle.

"When we came out here as children, it was my mother's painting studio. When us kids got too much she'd come out here for a bit of peace and quiet. She was really quite talented."

I smiled.

"Tea or coffee?"

"Tea, please," I said. "I can understand her needing a break. There were how many of you?"

Rascal let out a whistle. "There's five of us. FC, then Barry, then Sid, me, and baby Benedict."

"Wow," I said.

"I didn't understand it back then, why she'd ever need a break from us kids. Then I grew up. I can't sit near a table with kids on it for lunch without wanting a break," he muttered.

"But you have children. Your boys are wonderful."

"Harry's a pompous sack of useless knowledge, and Art... well, I just despair with that boy."

"You're hard on them. I think they're both really nice. I had a great chat with Art the other night."

"You did?"

I nodded. "He was telling me all about the book he's reading."

Rascal groaned. "That's all he ever wants to talk about. Me? I'm not a reader."

"You don't need to be a reader to just listen to him," I said.

"Hmm. I guess you're right. You take sugar?"

"Huh? Oh, no, thank you," I said.

"You're sweet enough, right? Sorry, I couldn't resist that one."

Rascal served the drinks and sat down across from me. I watched as he sipped his coffee right away, despite the temperature.

"So, what do you want to know?"

I decided to go right in with the biggest question I had. "What really happened out there?"

Rascal slapped his knee and laughed. "You really are a piece of work! I figured you'd start with some nice and easy getting to know you questions."

"I can do that if you'd prefer," I said.

"Alrighty."

"Tell me what it was like growing up as a Claus," I asked.

He leaned back in the chair. "Ah. Now that's the impossible question. I can only tell you what it was like for me. You see, every one of us had a different experience. I was baby number four, remember. It would take a whole load of bad luck for all three of my older brothers to pass away before any of them had a child."

"I'm not with you."

"That's the only way I'd ever have been Santa. It was never going to happen. So I had a very different upbringing than, say, FC, who always knew he was going to grow up and inherit the role. He had to be raised for it right from day one. His whole life was Christmas. I saw it, and I didn't envy it. By the time I came along, and then it was the same with Ben, we were never going to be Santa. We were encouraged to do our own thing, find our own interests."

"Did that bother you?"

"Never," he said emphatically. "Barry and Sid, they're the ones who had it rough. They were prepared for the role, too, but chances were always high they'd never be Santa. They were like those actors who wait around in case the actual actor gets sick."

"An understudy?" I asked.

"Heck, I don't know. I only know they exist because I was one for a school play once. I hated it. Learning all of those lines, getting the costume, doing the practice, just in case another kid was sick on the night? Of course, that kid wasn't sick. So I put in all of that work for nothing. No applause for me. No standing ovation. Imagine that being your whole life?"

"It must be really hard," I said. To my surprise, my mind jumped into the future, to a point where Nick and I might plan a family. Would my own children have that life? Would I want that for them?

"Ain't nothing that can be done about it," Rascal said with a shrug.

"It was Barry and Sid who found it hard?" I asked.

Rascal nodded.

"And Barry's passed away, I know that. What's the story with Sid?"

Rascal snorted. "Who knows. He's not been seen at a family event in years. He sends these cards explaining why he's far too busy to turn up to anything. Always goes on and on about his achievements and all of the important work he's doing. Actually, no. His secretary writes it out and sends it."

"He really must be busy."

"Very busy, or desperate for us to think he is."

"And what's the story with Benedict? He's the youngest, right?"

Rascal nodded. "My baby brother. Me and him were so close growing up. He was always a sickly kid. In and out of hospital. Lots of issues. I looked after him, made sure nobody ever picked on him at school. He never got better, really. Managed a career - something to do with books, I don't know - but gave that up when he got bad again."

"He sounds like Art, if he went into the literary world," I said with a smile.

Rascal looked at me. It was clear that thought had never crossed his mind. "Well, well. You just might have a point."

"Rascal, what was your issue with Norman? You didn't seem to get on with him."

"I downright dislike the fella, Holly. I don't mind telling you that."

"But why?"

"He's no good. Bitter, he is. I just couldn't really stand being around him. And it was such a shame, because Barry was a good man. Barry deserved a son with something more about him. He had no career plans. He had no interests. He was just... just a leech."

"You're definitely going to be the prime suspect if you speak like that to Wiggles," I warned.

Rascal shrugged. "I've always said it as it is, I'm not changing now."

"Okay," I said. We sat in silence for a few moments, sipping our drinks, lost in our private thoughts.

"Are you ready to tell me what happened out there?" I asked, finally.

Rascal shrugged. "There's nothing to tell. We split into pairs, I got the short straw and was stuck with Norman. He could ice fish, I'll say that about him. He was the short straw because I never had a word to say to him and I didn't want to spend all that time on my own with him. He was about as happy about it as I was, I reckon, because he kept trying to lose me. We found a hole, and I did make an effort with him, but it was like pulling teeth. One word answers, that kind of thing."

"Okay," I encouraged.

"We both caught a few. I know you're not interested in the fish side of things, but it was good fishing out there. The fish were just right there, under the ice. Sounds silly, but it's not always the case. Sometimes you wait hours for a catch or come back empty handed."

"But not this time?"

Rascal grinned. "It was like they were just lining up to get caught. So that helped pass the time. I mean, when there's no catches, all you have to do is wait so you want someone there who you can talk to. But we were so busy reeling them in, so that was lucky."

"But Norman seemed okay?"

"He seemed like he ever does. Did. He needed the loo an awful lot, I don't know if he had a water infection or something. In and out to the loo, which is not what you want out there... I mean, I don't want to get graphic with a lady, but you want to be keeping your trousers zipped as much as you can out there."

"And then back to Camp Walrus?"

Rascal nodded. "I was freezing at this point. That's the thing with catches, you can't just sit with your hands in your pockets if you're constantly reeling them in. So my hands were just frozen. I didn't say that to anyone, I didn't want to admit it like, but I was glad to get a hot tin of turkey curry in my hands to warm them up."

"This is the point where Norman left?"

"That's it. I'd sat down, got some grub in my hands, and I was telling everyone how good the fishing was. Norman upped and left, didn't even say a word to us. That's just like him. I mean, what kind of man wanders off into a snowstorm without so much as a goodbye?"

"Was he upset?" I asked.

Rascal shook his head. "No more than normal, anyway."

"There hadn't been any arguments? Any cross words? You hadn't... you hadn't..."

"Spit it out. In case you hadn't noticed, I'm impossible to offend."

"Had you offended him?"

15

I returned to Camp Mackerel and left Rascal in the log cabin washing the pots.

He had insisted that he hadn't offended Norman, although I wasn't sure that he'd really know if he had. Rascal was a charming man, but he wasn't sensitive to other people's feelings.

I'd found our conversation very enlightening, though, and I could see the pieces of this mystery falling into place a little more.

As soon as I pushed open the door to Camp Mackerel, Mrs Claus raced towards me.

"Holly, there you are! Come with me, now!" She called, her voice more urgent than I had ever heard it before.

"Nick?" I squeaked.

We asked a valet to sort a sleigh for us and swore them to secrecy about us leaving, and Mrs Claus expertly navigated her way across the ice and back to Candy Cane Hollow. I said nothing during the drive, partly so she could concentrate on the icy terrain, but mainly because I didn't think I wanted to know about whatever had happened.

To my horror, we pulled up outside the hospital and Mrs Claus broke into a jog across the car park. I dashed after her and tried to keep up with her as she navigated the twists and turns in the cavernous building.

"That way! Room 12!" a young nurse said as we approached, and we followed in the direction she pointed.

Mrs Claus pushed open the door to Room 12 and I gasped as I saw that the figure lying in the hospital bed was not Nick, not my beloved Nick, but Norman.

"You're alive?" I asked, even though the answer was obvious. There were wires attached and machines beeping, all proving that Norman was alive, even if his skin was a horrid colour and his body remained motionless.

An older nurse stole a glance at us without moving her head towards us. She was writing on a clipboard and said nothing to us, allowing us a private moment of shock.

"I can't believe it," I said.

"I know, dear!"

"He's in a critical condition. You won't be able to stay long. Please keep your voices down and don't overexcite him," the nurse said in a stern voice.

"Of course," I quickly agreed.

"He fell into a fishing hole," Mrs Claus said, her voice thick with emotion.

"That's awful. How did he get back out? Was he rescued?"

"We don't know. We just need him to wake up, dear, and then he can fill in some blanks for us. But the main thing is, he's safe."

"Why did you bring me here instead of Heidi?" I asked.

Mrs Claus pulled her gaze away from Norman and towards me. "I know that you're investigating, Holly."

I bristled. "Are you going to tell me not to?"

"Of course not, dear. I know that my husband already tried that. He does worry. He's been up all night fretting that you're going to get yourself hurt, you know."

I felt myself smile. "He has?"

Mrs Claus beamed at me. "Of course he has! You're part of the family, dear, and he does take this head of the family job a tad seriously."

"He's been worried about me?"

"Very much so. Why else would he ask you not to investigate?"

"Well, yeah," I said, not wanting to admit that my own thought process had been much more suspicious.

"Now, dear, I want you to stay safe, of course. But you're a natural when it comes to investigating. So I'm asking you to get back on the case. What do you think?"

"I actually never stopped investigating," I admitted.

Mrs Claus covered her ears and winked at me. "I didn't hear you, dear! Did you say you'll start again right away?"

I laughed and nodded my head. "Yes, that's exactly what I said."

"Wonderful. So, can I ask what you're thinking?"

"Well, Norman didn't fall," I said.

Mrs Claus nodded. "I thought you might say that."

"What's going to happen to him?" I asked, as I looked across at his lifeless frame, so weak and helpless, and smaller than it should be as he lay in the huge hospital bed.

"I don't know, dear. I don't know," Mrs Claus said, and she began to cry. I pulled her in to me and held her tight. I didn't shed a tear. My mind was racing.

The door pushed open and a doctor appeared. She wore her grey hair in a high bun, and had a stethoscope around her neck and a white coat over a gray blouse and black trousers.

"Mrs Claus, why don't you go and get us a drink? Let me speak to the doctor?" I asked.

In a daze, Mrs Claus nodded and walked out of the room.

"You're Holly Wood, right? I believe you're a GP. I can run through all of the medical lingo with you, if you want," the doctor said, her face impassive. I knew from experience that patients with medical knowledge were sometimes the easiest, and sometimes the hardest.

"Sure, that would be good. But first, can I ask you a question?"

Mrs Claus and I remained at the hospital, at Norman's bedside, overnight. We took an uncomfortable chair on either side of his bed, and not once did we feel how hard the seat padding was, never mind complain about it.

We didn't speak.

There was nothing to say.

The beep-beep-beep of the heart monitor was the rhythm we fell asleep to. It infiltrated our dreams. For me, it became the counting down of a microwave. The ticking of a clock. The low battery warning of a fire alarm. The indicator of my car.

A few minutes stolen away from reality, taken to a place where something as mundane as the counting down of a microwave could be on my mind.

I jolted awake, time and time again through the night, to remember where I was. To remember who was in the hospital bed by my side.

And then, morning came.

R IP NORMAN CLAUS: SECOND IN LINE TO SANTA ROLE IN FATAL FALL INTO FISHING HOLE

We are devastated to confirm that Norman Claus, 32, passed away yesterday following a fatal fall down a fishing hole.

Norman, currently the second in line to being Santa, after the current Santa-in-training Nick Claus, suffered terrible injuries.

A source close to the family explained:

"Norman was loved by everyone and his loss will devastate not only the Claus family, but the Candy Cane Hollow community as an entirety."

This publication exclusively revealed this week that Norman had an ongoing grudge with his cousin, Nick Claus, who was also present during the Claus' annual ice fishing trip.

It would seem that Nick is so caught up in his grief, he wasn't able to provide us with any comment.

While the entire Claus family declined to comment to this article, it is understood that the person now second in line is Heidi Claus, daughter of the late Barry Claus, although a misde-

meanour on her record from her teenage years may make her ineligible to become the next Santa.

Our source revealed:

"The Claus family are all devastated by the losses they have suffered this week. First Bella Baubles, a well-respected ice fishing guide, and now Norman. This will be a very different Christmas than the one everyone hoped for."

It is anticipated that an enquiry will be launched into the failings to secure the health and safety of all members of the annual Claus ice fishing party, and questions will have to be asked and answered regarding whether this dangerous hobby should continue to feature on the Claus calendar.

18

I returned to Camp Mackerel alone, via the back door.

The silence was overwhelming.

Gilbert glanced at me from the kitchen, then pretended he hadn't seen me. I was grateful. I didn't want to have to speak to him, or anyone else.

I pushed open the door to the den and kept my gaze down, unable to meet anyone's eyes.

Perched by the bar, I tried to ignore the thudding of my heart, the nerves about what I had to do.

"Drink?" Tomas asked.

I turned and nodded, gratefully.

"Oh, a cocoa please," I said.

He nodded and turned to work on my drink, then moved off to the side and picked up a crystal stemmed glass, took a discreet sip of a bubbly liquid.

"Are you allowed to drink on the job?" I asked with a smile.

"Oh, I never do, but I can't see a good bottle of champers go to waste. There were a few last dregs left. Besides, it's been quite the work week."

"You can say that again," I agreed.

Nick spotted me and came over, wrapped his arms around me.

"How are you doing?" I asked.

"I think I'm in shock. I guess we all are. Even Rascal hasn't got much to say. Are you okay?"

I nodded.

Tomas placed my cocoa down on the bar and I thanked him, then walked with Nick over to the main sitting area.

I offered a dull smile to all of the relatives who made eye contact with me. Heidi had been crying, Clive still was, and I could practically hear Gilbert howling from the kitchen.

The front door opened and a moment later, Mrs Claus walked in. She looked at me and gave me a small nod. Behind her, Wiggles hovered in the doorway.

"You don't need to tell us what happened to Norman, we've all read the paper," Rascal called across to him.

Wiggles' cheeks flushed.

"He's not here about that. He's here to arrest the killer," I said.

"What? You think it's one of us?" Heidi asked Wiggles.

"I'll explain," I said.

"Rascal, you've made no secret about the fact that you really dislike Norman. You hated being paired up with him on the fishing trip."

"Sure, I've admitted that all along."

"Wiggles and I always felt that Norman was too experienced to simply wander off and get lost. Something must have happened to him. You were the prime suspect, Rascal."

"So I gather."

"You should never have let Norman leave Camp Walrus, not even for a moment. But what I thought was curious was that as soon as Father Christmas made a move to follow Norman, you got up right away. Because that was your golden opportunity, right? You had to wait a minute, so you could go back in and say you hadn't found him."

Rascal made a show of yawning into his hand. "I didn't find him."

"It would only take a minute to find that open hole and push him in. The snow and the cold would swallow up any scream he had time for, the splash of him falling in," I said.

"And why would I want to have pushed him in?"

"That was the thing I stumbled over. What could your motive have been? Normally, if it's just that you hate a person so much you want to kill them, you're not quite so vocal about it. And you have been very vocal about disliking Norman."

"I'm vocal about everything. Now, are you accusing me of murder? Because that might just affect your chances of me wanting that date with you."

I smiled. "No, Rascal, you're not the murderer. But I still don't want that date, thank you."

Rascal shrugged, as if it was no real loss to him.

"So, who did it?" Heidi asked.

"Who did what?" I asked.

Heidi furrowed her brows. "Who killed my brother? This isn't a game, Holly."

"I know it isn't. Forgive me. It will all make sense. And, I'll admit, I had to treat you as a suspect, Heidi."

Her cheeks flushed and I saw some of her strong facade crack. "Me? You think I could have hurt him?"

"He was an obstacle between you and being Santa. So was Nick. When the attempt on Nick's life was made..."

"The icicle," Heidi gasped. "The icicle made me a suspect."

I nodded. "With Norman and Nick both out of the picture, you would have been the next Santa."

"That's true," Father Christmas said.

"But I've never wanted to be Santa. I have my life. I'm studying," Heidi protested.

"You're studying the patriarchy. Being the first female Santa would be an amazing way to turn those theories into real life practice," I said.

Rascal groaned. "Heidi's no killer. Anyone can see that."

"Thanks, uncle," she said with a faint smile.

"I read the newspaper," I said. "Heidi, is it true what it said about you?"

Heidi shrugged lazily. "I don't know, probably. I don't even care. That's the last thing on my mind."

"But you do have something on your record?"

"Maybe you should talk about this in private," Mrs Claus suggested.

Heidi batted that suggestion away. "It's fine. It's hardly a secret - it's in the newspaper! I had a couple of wild years as a teenager, a few drunk and disorderly issues, nothing major."

"Nothing major for lots of people. For a Claus, it's a different story," Father Christmas explained.

"Guys, I don't care. I have my life. I've not been waiting around hoping I get a chance to be the next Santa. And I have no history of violence, if that's what you're thinking. I know I can be a bit, well, mouthy, but I've never hurt a soul in my life."

"I know you haven't," I said.

"So I'm not a suspect?" Heidi asked.

"No, you're not. And when I got to this point of my investigation, I realised I was forgetting an important part of things."

Nick swallowed. "What was that?"

"Do you remember Nick, I told you that I felt sorry for Bella. That poor woman. She'd got herself wrapped up in a Claus calamity and paid the price with her life. Even the newspaper articles barely mentioned her."

Father Christmas looked down at the floor. "Holly's right. We've been so wrapped up in our own grief, we've barely thought about that poor woman. Oh, nutcracker! I haven't even called her next of kin and passed on our condolences. Her poor family must be beside themselves."

"Oh, you can pass on your condolences to her next of kin now," I said.

Father Christmas looked up at me curiously. "I shall, Holly, but please, I'll let you finish first."

"Thank you. I was looking at it all wrong. It turns out, this is all about Bella. The Claus family got tied up in something, and Norman paid with his life."

"What are you saying?" Heidi asked.

"I'm saying that Bella was killed. That was pre-meditated. Killing an ice fishing guide isn't that hard to plan, since they don't routinely follow the rule about working in pairs."

"Rule 43B(A)," Wiggles clarified.

"Thanks," I shot him a grateful look.

"We've explained why we don't work in pairs! It's one of those rules made up by someone who sits in an office and never goes out on the ice!" Salty chimed in.

"Its okay. I'm not here to say that Bella did anything wrong," I reassured him.

"Who would want to hurt Bella? She seemed like such a sweetheart," Rascal said.

Heidi rolled her eyes. "You barely knew her."

"She was a sweetheart," Salty said.

"Tell us about her," I asked.

Salty cleared his throat. "She was only 22 years old, generations of ice fishing in her blood, more skilled at tracking and finding fish than she had any right to be. Didn't always make her popular on the ice, lot of older folks thought she hadn't put in the hours to get as good as she was."

"So she had enemies?" Rascal asked.

Salty glared at the punk rocking Claus. "Nobody, absolutely nobody, in the ice fishing world, would push another guide into a hole. Don't matter out there whether you love a person or hate them, you only survive if you have each other's backs."

"It's an honourable profession," Father Christmas said.

Salty nodded. "Thank you, sir."

"No, Bella wasn't killed by a professional colleague. She was killed because of love, not hate. Or maybe love that's become hate. Some people say that love and hate are close to each other, but I've never believed that. What I do believe, is that Bella was killed for falling out of love."

"A crime of passion?" Heidi asked with a gasp.

I nodded. "She was a young woman exploring her options. She'd been in a relationship, but that relationship wasn't working for her anymore. So she ended it. And a new man caught her eye. Maybe he'd caught her eye all along."

"Norman," Heidi whispered.

"You noticed her flirting with him. I saw it too. It's funny how flirting seems to be a universal language, but men often don't see it. Maybe Norman didn't pick up on it, or maybe he was unsure how he felt. He was ten years older than Bella, after all."

"What does that matter?" Rascal jeered.

"I'm not saying it matters at all. The two of them could

have lived happily ever after perhaps, if not for her jealous ex."

A bitter laugh came from the room and I turned, finally, to look at the killer.

"Tomas, you couldn't stand to see her move on, could you?" I asked.

Everyone turned to look at the barman, who stood behind the bar with his arms folded, a smirk of arrogance on his face.

"So we hooked up once or twice. Who cares?" He said.

"It was more than that, Tomas. Do you remember last year? You and I sat up late one night talking. You told me you were going to propose," Nick said.

"That's why you asked him right away whether Bella was still here when we arrived?" I asked.

Nick nodded. "They were a pair in my head. Tomas and Bella; Bella and Tomas."

"Well, not anymore," Tomas sneered.

"You remembered all of that, dear? Oh, how wonderful! See, you'll be a marvellous Santa!" Mrs Claus beamed.

"You managed to sneak out and stalk her, didn't you? Were you planning to kill her, or did you only decide that when you saw her with another man?" I asked.

Tomas rolled his eyes. "I didn't leave here. And why would I care about her and Norman? She was practically throwing herself at him, making it so obvious that she liked him. It was pathetic."

"Hold on! That's why he kept going to the toilet? The sly dog was sneaking off to be with Bella?! Wow. I'm starting to like Norman, I'll admit it," Rascal exclaimed.

"That's what I think. Except, that last time he snuck off when you were all eating, was just as Tomas had arrived."

Tomas laughed. "And you have evidence?"

I turned to Wiggles and nodded at him. He left the room and walked into the seldom used library.

"You follow the news?" I asked Tomas.

"Sure. So what?" Tomas exclaimed.

"It turns out, Tomas, you can leak stories to the newspaper. Even if those stories aren't true. In fact, you know all this. Because you've been creating the news. You called and gave the newspaper the tip about Nick having a grudge against Norman."

Tomas rolled his eyes. "Sure, from out here where I'm surrounded by Claus relatives. As if I'd even have the time to kill, never mind the time to actually kill."

"Watch your tone, Tomas," Father Christmas warned.

Gilbert huffed. "You've got all the time in the world now I'm running your kitchen."

"You planted suspicion that Nick might have killed Norman. But nobody really took that seriously, did they? The police didn't come out here and arrest him."

"You're not listening. I have no idea about any of this."

"You know the advantage of being good waiting staff? You become invisible. I was told that years ago, that a good bar person or waiter should disappear into the background, barely even be noticed," I said.

"Somebody forgot to tell Gilbert that!" Clive joked.

Heidi gasped and covered her mouth. "The icicle?"

"The icicle."

"How would I even target an icicle at Nick?" Tomas asked.

"That's a good question. I don't think you did. I think you'd have been happy for that icicle to hurt whoever next walked in to the kitchen. You wanted everyone scared and suspecting each other, because you needed the Claus family to be the focus, not Bella. It was just chance that it was Nick who got hurt."

"Hold on, how do you even know about the icicle if it wasn't you who did it?" Rascal asked.

Tomas let out a splutter. "Someone told me about it. It must have been Denzel."

"I don't think so," Denzel said, his arms folded.

"The quiet one who reads then, I don't know. What does it matter?"

"I don't think you even wanted to kill anyone with the icicle. It was just a warning. Just a way of getting everyone scared." I said. My voice quivered and Heidi leaned over and squeezed my hand.

"Why on earth would I..."

"Because you had to make sure that Bella's death was just a byline. You had to keep the investigation focused on the Claus family, on one of them being a killer."

"Great theory, but I still don't see any evidence," Tomas said.

"The evidence will see you locked up and the key thrown away. You might as well get your side of the story heard."

Tomas glanced around the room, then the cocky smile returned to his face.

"Fine. I did it. I'd had enough of Bella flirting with him right in front of my face. She thought she was so swell, catching the eye of an older man. It was ridiculous."

"So you decided to kill her?"

Tomas shrugged. "Why not? We both made promises, you know. I promised I'd never hurt her again. She promised she wouldn't leave me."

"You'd hurt her before?" I asked, stunned.

"Nothing major. She was out of the hospital in a day or

two. She knew how to push my buttons, that's the thing. But we were working past it. She was behaving better. Then I got home from work one day and all of her stuff was gone. No goodbye letter, nothing."

"But she carried on working here," I said, my voice low.

"She didn't exactly have a lot of other options. Ice fishing guide was all she knew. She was applying, though. I was running out of time. I knew she'd come back to me. At least, until she met him."

"Norman?"

"She probably saw him as her way to the fast life. She was probably dumb enough to think he'd be Santa. Heck, I'd be a better Santa."

"You'll never go near the costume," Father Christmas rose to his feet, his expression perfectly calm.

Tomas laughed. "And what's the alternative? Heidi over there with her criminal record? Sid the pharma king who can't even be bothered to come to your get togethers? Every year I stand here and listen to you say how sad it is that he can't be here! Oh, wait - Rascal! There's the answer! Ha! In case you haven't noticed, your family is running low on suitable Santas. And Norman's little romance with a member of staff won't look good, not the way I can spin a headline to the press. So let's just pipe down with all of this and move on. I did what was necessary."

"Tomas," Wiggles said.

"Shut up! I'm talking. You are all going to start listening. Now, I'm a fair man. I don't want to ruin you all if I don't have to. So I'm going to just slip away now, and we'll all move on with our lives."

"Tomas," Wiggles repeated.

Tomas closed his eyes and let out a long breath. "You need to stop interrupting me, old man."

"Tomas."

The voice caused everyone to stop and stare at the doorway, where Norman stood. He was on crutches, and his nose had been stitched up, but he was there. Norman Claus, alive and kind of well.

I rose and went to him, helped him into a seat.

"Welcome home," Father Christmas said.

"You're alive?" Tomas asked. He looked as if he had seen a ghost.

"Remind me, Harry, what do the court think about attempted murders?" Nick asked.

Harry puffed out his chest, happy to help out. "They sentence them the same as the full crime."

"Ah, interesting. So it's a long future in Candy Cane Custody, if I'm right, for one murder and one attempted murder."

"You're right, indeed. Tomas Tinsel, I'm arresting you on suspicion of murder, attempted murder and perverting the course of justice."

Wiggles strode across the room, but Tomas was quick and dashed through the door into the kitchen.

"After him!" Wiggles called out.

I grinned and held up the back door key. "Don't worry, he's not going far."

19

We all followed Wiggles into the kitchen, to see him scratching his head. The room was empty, apart from Gilbert, who was stirring a huge pan of hot cocoa.

"Well, I'll be darned. He's disappeared."

"But how? I locked the door," I said.

"There must be another way out. Everyone search!" Wiggles ordered.

We each picked a corner of the room and began searching for Tomas. He was a big, strong guy - strong enough to push Bella and Norman into the fishing hole - but desperation could make a big person try to hide in a tiny space.

We checked cupboards, behind the vacuum cleaner, and did a thorough inspection of the pantry, all while Gilbert continued perfecting the cocoa recipe. Rascal insisted on doing check of the garden, even though the kitchen door hadn't been unlocked.

Twenty minutes later, we hadn't found a sign of him.

"Well, Lords a leaping! Where the heck has Tomas gone?" Wiggles asked.

"Tomas?" Gilbert asked.

"Yes, he came running right in here. That's who we've been searching for."

"Oh! You should have said! I tossed that slovenly turkey-muncher in the blast freezer," Gilbert said with a wink.

We all burst into laughter as Wiggles pulled open the door, and a half-frozen Tomas waddled out.

"Gilbert! What a thing to do," I said between giggles.

"What do you know, the elf's starting to grow on me too," Rascal said with a grin.

Gilbert watched his freezing nemesis with his nose turned up. "Holly, dear, I've been wanting to do that to him ever since we arrived. Would you believe, he was using non-seasonal tea towels in here?!"

I pulled the elf in for a hug and we all cheered as Wiggles escorted Tomas out to police custody, complete with an extra loud blast of *Last Christmas* on repeat for the drive to Candy Cane Custody.

**

Gilbert finished making cocoa for everyone, as they all checked on Norman and fussed over his injuries.

"I want to say thank you. I know I asked a lot of you all, going along with pretending Norman was dead. I just knew that Tomas would feel extra cocky if he felt there wasn't a surviving witness."

"And we had to get justice for poor Bella, dears," Mrs Claus said.

"It had to be done," Rascal said.

"We're all natural liars, it turns out. Maybe my criminal record is more easily explained than I'd realised," Heidi said with a grin.

"I'm guessing that Tomas was Bella's next of kin?" Father Christmas said.

I nodded. "I heard him on the phone. It didn't mean much at the time but it came back to me later. I realised the call was the police informing him. He was surprised, on the call. I think Bella must have forgotten to update her records."

"It's so very sad. I'm pleased that her parents have been informed now," Mrs Claus said.

We all agreed, and sat in silence for a moment as we thought about her parents receiving that dreadful call.

"How are you holding up? I know this must be hard," I asked Norman.

Norman shrugged. "It was early days. It might have just fizzled out."

"You should have told us about her, dear. She seemed like a lovely young lady."

"Young being the right word! You were punching above your weight, Norman!" Rascal exclaimed.

Norman smiled. "I know that. She'd have soon realised that she could do better."

"Don't put yourself down. You're not that bad," Rascal said.

"Is that a compliment you're giving someone?" Art asked. He was in the familiar corner of the room, his nose in a different book with a cover that looked almost identical to the last one.

"You know, Art, I was hoping you'd take me book shopping one day."

Art lowered his book and looked at his father, clearly waiting for a punch line.

"I'm serious. It's about time we spent some proper time

together. I'm thinking you take me to a book shop, and I'll get us lunch after."

Art grinned. It was a slow, self-conscious smile and I ached for the awkward teen years he was stuck in. No doubt he'd mature and find his fellow book lovers and probably land a career that amazed us all. Youth could be cruel. But it passed. And he would grow into himself, I was sure.

"Okay, dad. Sure. I can do that."

"Well, that's that, then. And no, Harry, you're not getting a similar offer. I'm being bled dry by your university fees."

Harry grinned. "That's fine, dad."

"So, what happens now?" I asked.

Gilbert cleared his throat. "If it's not too much trouble, perhaps you could all make your way to the dining room. I've had a beef joint sitting in its own juices for far too long. I've never served a dry joint in all my life and I don't intend to start now!"

We all laughed.

"Good to know that some things are unchanged," I said.

20

I slipped into my kitten heels by the front door of Claus Cottage and took a deep breath, tried to steady my nerves as I waited for Mrs Claus to finish getting ready.

Suddenly, I felt a presence behind me and turned to see Nick, his gaze focused on me and a beaming smile on his cute face.

"Hey, you," I said, breathy.

"Wow. You look incredible, Holly," he said.

I giggled, grateful for the compliment but not sure how to respond. I decided to go for silly, and did a quick little twirl. The skirt of my off the shoulder red dress fanned out around me and I felt like a little girl preparing for a party.

"Is it okay? I wasn't sure what style to go for," I fumbled as my confidence dipped.

Tonight was the Mistletoe Matchmakers event, and I was nervous about taking such a public role with Mrs Claus. I knew that the eyes of the Candy Cane Hollow community would be on me, watching and wondering what my involvement meant.

I'd already heard hushed rumours about my wedding to Nick - a wedding that neither of us had discussed, never mind started planning!

The whole town wanted a wife for Nick, and I could hardly deny that I was on the same page with them, but I didn't want to be rushed. And I didn't want to let anyone down.

"Hey?" Nick squeezed my hand.

"Huh? Sorry, I was miles away," I admitted.

He grinned. "I'm boring you already."

"No, no, I guess some of the pressures of your family are just sinking in with me a little. How do you deal with it?" I asked.

Nick shrugged. "I've never known different. It's always been the same for me. You should ask my mum, since she, erm, married into it."

His cheeks flushed and I realised that all of the thoughts racing around my head were also whipping around his. I also realised that he would never propose while I appeared to have worries about the public side of being his wife.

I gulped and nodded my head. "That's a good idea. I'll ask Mrs Claus."

"Ask me what, dear? Oh! Holly! You look as perfect as a decorated Christmas tree!"

"Thanks," I said with an awkward smile as I turned to see Mrs Claus come down the staircase. She looked incredible in a full-length black gown with a glittery red shrug to keep her arms warm.

"You look beautiful, mum," Nick said.

"You really do. Wow," I agreed.

Mrs Claus batted away the compliments. "Thank you, dears. It does feel wonderful to get dressed up for a fun night out. Oh, Holly, I'm so excited about tonight! We're going to help people feel less alone, right in time for Christmas! Isn't that splendid?"

"It really is," I said with a grin.

I kissed Nick goodbye and headed out with Mrs Claus to one of the grander sleighs. We were just about to pull away when the front door to Claus Cottage opened and Gilbert ran out, a foil-wrapped package in his hands.

"Mrs Claus! Mrs Claus! I made you a snack for the journey!" He called as he jogged across to the sleigh in his pointy-toed slippers.

"Oh, Gilbert, you shouldn't have!" Mrs Claus exclaimed.

He stopped in his tracks, a couple of feet away from the sleigh. "I shouldn't have? What does that mean? Oh! I understand. You saw this event as a way to avoid eating a meal from Gilbert's kitchen, and jumped at the chance! And you, too, Holly? I see. I see. You'll be able to tell people tonight that I sent you out on hungry stomachs! That's enough to ruin my career! Ruin my reputation! Why, I've got half a mind to hang up my..."

"Gilbert?" Mrs Claus interrupted.

"Yes?" He asked.

"We'd love to accept the snacks. That's very kind, dear. Now, please go back inside before those slippers let in the snow and give you hypothermia."

Gilbert glanced down at his feet, realised his mistake, and practically threw the package at us before running back indoors.

We looked at each other and smiled as the sleigh began its journey through the snow-filled streets into the town centre.

"Well, dear, what did you want to ask me?" Mrs Claus asked.

I felt my cheeks flushed. "Oh, well. I. I just wondered

how you'd adjusted to life as Mrs Claus."

Mrs Claus grinned bigger and brighter than I'd ever seen before, and rubbed her hands together in glee.

"There's no particular reason why I'm wanting to know. Nothing's, erm, nothing's happened," I fumbled, not wanting to let her imagine that Nick had proposed.

She gave me an exaggerated wink. "Of course not, it's just general curiosity. Sure, sure. Well, Holly, I realised that the people of Candy Cane Hollow are good and kind people. They're interested in the Claus family, how could they not be? But they wish us all well. It's like having tens of thousands of close friends!"

I swallowed. That sounded nice, I had to admit, but also kind of intimidating.

"You seem so good at remembering everyone's names and arranging these amazing events," I said.

"Ah. Holly, try to remember how long I've been Mrs Claus. I'll bet you weren't half the doctor you are now on your first day. I'll bet your bedside manner has got better, and you can find a vein to take blood easier, and you can refer a poorly patient to the hospital in a way that doesn't panic them?"

I thought back to my early days in my career and winced. "I was awful in the early days. I'd sit down with patients and be so desperate to show them that I knew what I was doing, I'd speak in jargon and completely confuse them. They didn't understand a word I was saying."

"And now?" Mrs Claus asked.

"Well... I guess I've relaxed into it more. Relaxed into myself more as well."

Mrs Claus nodded. "I couldn't have said it better myself, dear."

The sleigh pulled up at Vixen's Village Hall, venue for

the Mistletoe Matchmakers, and the elf driver climbed down and offered a hand to help us out.

The building was small and quaint, but decorated with twinkly lights. A line of people snaked around the perimeter, and they began to cheer as they saw that we had arrived.

Mrs Claus waved at everyone as we walked by the line and towards the entrance. I watched her, took a deep breath, and did the same.

"Oh, dears! We're so excited to see you all! We'll get set up and get these doors open as quick as we can!" Mrs Claus gushed.

"Holly! Holly!" A young voice called out from the crowd. I turned to see a girl, perhaps six years old, standing with her mother. I couldn't resist, and went over to her.

"Hello there," I said as I crouched down to remove the height difference. "Are you here for matchmakers?"

The girl laughed at me. "No, silly. We came to see you."

"You did?" I asked, with a glance towards her mum.

The woman smiled at me and nodded, then gave an encouraging fuss of her daughter's golden hair.

"Tell Holly why you wanted to see her."

The girl looked up at me, and I found that I couldn't have looked away from her almond eyes if I'd wanted to.

"When I grow up, I want to be a doctor just like you," she said with a puff of pride.

I grinned. "Well, that's excellent. We need more great doctors and I can see that you will be a great doctor. What's your name?"

"Amelia," she said.

"Well, Amelia, if your mummy wants to call the surgery next week, I'm sure we can book in a tour for you. Let you see some of the equipment I have."

"Really? Wow! Awesome! Can we, mummy?"

The woman grinned and mouthed 'thank you' to me, then picked Amelia up and held her tight. "We sure can, kiddo."

I said a goodbye to them and made my way into the village hall. Mrs Claus had already opened the doors and most of the queue of people had worked their way inside.

Mrs Claus stood on the stage, chatting to a young woman about the timing of the music and lighting. It was amazing to see how involved Mrs Claus was in the small details for the event.

I looked out at the crowd of people, all eagerly stood at the back of the room, waiting to be randomly assigned a partner for the first round of speed dating. There were people of all ages, elves and humans, all sporting the energy of nervous excitement. I felt myself share their emotions. They were just a few hours away from possibly leaving with a new love interest, a new friend... the possibilities were endless.

The young assistant left the stage and I moved closer to Mrs Claus as the lights dimmed.

"Ready, dear?"

"I can't wait," I admitted.

Mrs Claus cleared her throat, and the room immediately grew silent. "Welcome everyone to Mistletoe Matchmakers! This is truly one of my favourite events of the year, because it's a reminder to us all that strangers are simply friends we haven't met yet. And sometimes more than friends! I'm delighted to be hosting this event with Dr Holly Wood!"

The crowd applauded and I looked out and saw their beaming faces and felt pure, simple joy.

I hadn't planned to, but I leaned in to my own microphone to say a few words. "I'm very excited to be here tonight with Mrs Claus. As most of you will know, I'm a newcomer to this special community. I wanted to take part in this event because I remember how unsure I felt about moving to this new place and meeting new people. And I remember how much I was welcomed by you all. Now, let's do some matchmaking!"

A loud whistle came from the audience and I looked down and saw Ginger in a figure hugging silver catsuit. I grinned at her and waved. Near her, in a very dapper black tie suit, was Wiggles. I gave him a wave too. As I spotted more and more familiar faces in the audience, I realised that Candy Cane Hollow truly was home.

The night was a huge success. I couldn't imagine that a single person hadn't left without making at least one new friend. A few couples seemed to particularly hit it off, and more than one pair left the event arm in arm, all whispers and fluttered eyelashes as they headed out into the night.

"Well, dear. You were marvellous!"

"Thank you! You were too! What a night!"

"Doesn't it feel good to do something so special for the community, dear?"

I smiled, as I realised that it had. I'd enjoyed every second.

"The sleigh's here for us, dear," Mrs Claus said.

"I'm going to take a walk back, actually," I said.

Mrs Claus walked to the back of the stage, where a coat stand was, and pulled down a huge winter coat. She held it up and I obediently pushed my arms into it.

Once she was happy that I was warm enough for the walk home, she gave me a kiss on the cheek and said good night.

The night air was crisp, but not too frigid. Snow fell and the streets were quiet. I was alone in a winter wonderland, and on a high from the successful night's event.

I pulled out my phone and dialled before I could change my mind.

"Holly! It's so good to hear from you! Wait, wait a second. Tom? Can you take Jeb? It's Holly!" August chattered away after answering on the first dial. I heard a commotion as she handed baby Jeb to her handsome husband, and then a click of a door closing, and quiet.

"Is it a bad time?" I asked. I knew how busy my sister's life was, as a wife and a parent and a homemaker.

She laughed. "Are you kidding me? I was just sat scrolling on my phone killing time until Jeb goes to bed. It's been one of those days!"

I felt my heart lurch. I was so quick to imagine that August's life was perfect.

"Is everything okay?"

"Sure, sure! It's fine. Anyway, how are things with you? How's Mr Hunkalicious?"

I cringed. Nick would never be called anything different by my sister, I just knew it.

"He's really good. I've just been out for the evening with his mum, actually."

"Wooing the mother in law? Wow. You really must be keen," August teased.

"She's really sweet. Nick jokes that I'm only with him because of her."

"He jokes and has a pretty face. Tell me again why you haven't married him yet?"

"Oh, I'm not thinking about that yet. We're just enjoying each day."

"You truly are the sensible one! Hey, what's the weather like there? I'm hoping for a white Christmas, as always, but it's not looking likely."

I looked out at the snow covered fields as I walked up the hill towards Claus Cottage. "It's snowing here."

"It's always snowing there! It's like you've moved to some winter wonderland, sis."

I laughed. "It really is. You have to see this place to believe it. In fact..."

"What?"

"I know this is early, and you probably need to check with Tom and whatever, but do you want to spend next Christmas with me here? All of you, of course."

There was a pause and I wondered if I had made a mistake. How on earth would I explain Candy Cane Hollow to my sister?

"You're kidding? Holly, yes! We'd love to!"

"Yay! Well, put it in your diary! I'm so pleased."

A wail came from August's end of the phone, a hushed apology, a groan from my sister. "Sorry, Hol, Jeb's fussing for me. Like I said, one of those days. But let's speak again soon, yeah? And I'm putting next Christmas in my diary right now!"

I laughed and said goodbye.

I could see a commotion up at Claus Cottage and realised that I'd almost missed Nick's relatives all leaving. The sleighs and cars were overflowing with suitcases and the travel snacks that Gilbert had made for everyone.

I picked up my pace, keen to return and get to say goodbye to everyone.

"Hey, here she comes! You look in a hurry, lady. Let me guess, you want me to take your number after all?" Rascal teased as I reached the house, a little out of breath.

I grinned and pulled him into a bear hug. His bark was worse than his bite, and the old punk was growing on me.

"It's been so good to meet you, Holly! Now remember,

just give us a little notice so we can buy hats, okay?!" Clive said as he pulled me in for a hug.

Denzel tutted by his side. "Don't listen to this old romantic. It's been great to meet you!"

"You too!"

Heidi came over and rolled her eyes. "We are so outnumbered by all of these stinking men. You better make sure that you and Nick have daughters, okay?"

I flushed and changed the subject. "So they can battle the patriarchy?"

Heidi laughed. "Lords a leaping, no! So they can help us keep the bathrooms cleaner!"

I laughed as Harry offered me a handshake and Art gave me a quick nod of his head.

Norman was the last to leave Claus Cottage, and he pulled me into a tight hug. "Thanks for everything, Holly. Welcome to the family."

I pulled back and smiled at him. He was hurting, but his heart would mend.

"Same time next year?" Father Christmas asked as everyone piled back into their vehicles.

Mumbled shouts of agreement came back in reply.

Nick reached for me and I leaned in and planted a kiss on his lips. His dimple winked at me until I closed my eyes.

I knew that Mrs Claus was watching.

I knew his whole family was watching.

And I didn't mind at all.

THE END

Extend your stay in Candy Cane Hollow
Book Four: Mistletoe Murder
mybook.to/christmas4

CHRISTMAS MYSTERY BONUSES

Help yourself to a festive fun pack, available exclusively at:

https://dl.bookfunnel.com/9ckxf7kcfh

Ho-ho-hope you enjoy it!

Mona x

ABOUT THE AUTHOR

Mona Marple is a lover of all things book-related. When she isn't working on her next release, she's probably curled up somewhere warm reading a good story.

Mona is a fan of all things festive and is looking forward to adding to the Christmas Cozy Mystery series over the years. Her other cozy mysteries include the Waterfell Tweed series, the Mystic Springs paranormal series, the co-written A Witch In Time paranormal series, and the Mexican Mysteries series.

Mona lives in Nottinghamshire, England with her bread baking husband, her always-singing daughter, and their pampered Labradoodle, Coco. In fact, Mona's online reader group were a big part of persuading Mona's husband to welcome Coco into their home!

facebook.com/monamarpleauthor

instagram.com/monamarple